WORLD OF THERMO:
THERMOMETER RISING

By Guy Walton
With Nick Walker

Illustrated by Alyssa Josue

Green Blob Publishing
Smyrna, GA

Follow Guy on Twitter @ClimateGuyW
Read Guy's blog at GuyOnClimate.com

DEDICATION

I would like to dedicate this book to my father, The Reverend Guy Walton Senior, who gave me a great moral upbringing and taught me the discipline to accomplish my goal of becoming a meteorologist. He also demonstrated the perseverance I needed to do my climate research.

I also dedicate this book to my mother Ruby Myers Walton who home-schooled me through much of the early elementary grades due to my childhood asthma and bronchitis. She was a wonderful mom her entire life.

I also want to dedicate this book to Dr. Raymond Staley, who is in his nineties and living in chilly North Dakota. Dr. Staley was a professor of Oceanography and Meteorology at Florida State University where I earned my meteorology degree, and he was a valuable mentor during my years at FSU in the early 80s.

Finally, I would like to dedicate this book to the late Dr. Charles David Keeling and his son Ralph Keeling for their tireless efforts at measuring the levels of atmospheric carbon dioxide over the Earth.

Praise for
World of Thermo: Thermometer Rising

"One of the biggest questions I get is, 'How do I talk to my kids about climate change?' This book is the answer - it takes us on an entertaining trip through time, to meet the scientists who've studied our planet and what makes it tick." – Dr. Katharine Hayhoe, Director of Climate Science Center, Texas Tech University

"One of the great ironies of human-caused climate change is that those who had the least role in causing it—our children—will bear the brunt of its devastating impacts if we fail to act in time. It is urgent that they be educated about the threat and that their voices be heard. *World of Thermo* uses engaging magical characters to bring the science alive, and inform while entertaining." – Dr. Michael E. Mann, Distinguished Professor of Atmospheric Science, Penn State University, and co-author of *The Madhouse Effect,* and *The Tantrum that Saved the World.*

"*World of Thermo* is a highly entertaining and superbly illustrated look at climate change and meteorology by an exceptionally well-qualified atmospheric scientist. Guy Walton takes readers on a wonderfully imaginative ride through climatological history as well as providing a learned peek into the disquieting future." – H. W "Buzz" Bernard, author of *Eyewall, Supercell,* and *Cascadia*

"The saga of global climate change is full of twists and turns, invisible agents, all-too-human actors, and some very complex science. In *World of Thermo,* meteorologist/writer Guy Walton and illustrator Alyssa Josue turn this journey into a compelling tale for bright young readers that brings more than a century of climate science and awareness to life." – Robert Henson, author of *The Thinking Person's Guide to Climate Change*

CONTENTS

ACKNOWLEDGMENTS

A special thanks to the following people who helped me on this journey:

To Nick Walker the Weather Dude® for his edits, rewrites and creative ideas, taking us both back to our childhoods in the process.

To Dr. Michael E. Mann, Dr. Katharine Hayhoe, Buzz Bernard and Bob Henson for their knowledge, expertise and support.

To Bernadette Woods Placky of Climate Central, Dr. Greg Forbes and Tom Niziol of The Weather Channel, and tropical expert Michael Lowry for taking time to review several stories for accuracy.

I would also like to extend my heartfelt appreciation to Linda Dean Starkey, Marsha Walton, Peter Van DeNeng, Barbara Walker, Yashar Karayunusoglu, Yavuz Alicioglu, and John Hartwell for helping me to mentally and physically cope during an extremely difficult period of my life.

FOREWORD

Ever since Dr. James Hansen's testimony before Congress in 1988, I have observed the struggle experts have endured in convincing Americans about the urgency of the global warming/climate issue. One reason for that is because carbon dioxide is a faceless, odorless, colorless gas. That faceless gas has increased in the atmosphere due to the burning of fossil fuels, while at the same time, average temperatures have risen dramatically over the Earth, especially since the beginning of the 21st century. Even so, there are still enough cold weather events every winter to cause intelligent people to believe that climate change is either not occurring, or is of minor importance. Add to that the habit of humans to act only on what seems urgent, plus our tendency to largely accept information that confirms our preexisting beliefs, and we end up generally ignoring the biggest environmental problem facing the world today.

World of Thermo: Thermometer Rising is a tale for young people that addresses the problem. It is the fantastical story of Thermo the Flying Thermometer, a magical creation who interacts with clouds, storms and humans to help save humanity from a terrible plight of its own making. His enemy Carbo, a twisted carbon dioxide molecule, tries to convince humans that global warming is not a problem in order to help his other carbon dioxide friends. As his friends turn out to be more dangerous than anyone knows, Carbo's good intentions vanish, and he becomes the "face of evil" in the modern climate world. The fight between Thermo and Carbo represents the struggle of science and reason to overcome shortsighted apathy and greed.

The stories in this collection chronicle some of the major climate and weather events from the Industrial Revolution to the 21st century. After each chapter is a short section explaining the parallels in the story to "real world" events. At the end of the book is an Appendix with further details about each historical event, as well as more scientific explanations and personal observations. In *World of Thermo: Thermometer Rising* I have presented climatologists and meteorologists as heroes, particularly those whom I have personally known in my thirty-plus year career at The Weather Channel.

I hope you enjoy the stories and will be enlightened.

Guy Walton

STORY 1: THERMO FLIES

In a secret laboratory at the base of Mauna Loa Volcano in Hawaii, Dr. Emmanuel Key bent over a sample of air he had collected from the outside. A climate scientist, Dr. Key had collected such samples for the past three years, measuring the concentrations of various gases in each one.

"Mm," mumbled Dr. Key as he checked his readings. "It is still increasing."

Since he started his measurements, the doctor had noticed a gradual rise in the amount of carbon dioxide, or CO_2 in the atmosphere around Mauna Loa. Though he knew the odorless and colorless gas existed in the air naturally, the growing concentrations no longer seemed completely natural to him.

Mauna Loa was the perfect setting for Dr. Key's research. Far away from factories and automobiles, the doctor could get reliable readings in the pristine air. The location also allowed him to build living quarters inside a deep cave within the volcano. Dr. Key, having some quirks that people of high intelligence often do, furnished the cave with 19th century Edwardian décor, with colorful Persian rugs on the floors and beautiful old oil paintings on the walls. The ornate surroundings created a curious contrast to the glass tubes, measuring equipment and electronic gadgetry that otherwise occupied his home.

Dr. Key did not live there alone. "Joshua, please come here," the doctor called to his butler. Dr. Key didn't really have an official butler, but one of the technicians he employed had, over time, become his assistant with household chores and errands.

"Yes, Dr. Key?" Joshua answered as he sprinted into the room.

"As you know," began the doctor, "I have been collecting carbon dioxide samples for three years, and now it's time for my next move. I'd like to build my own personal reconnaissance flying machine that can measure the Earth's temperature."

"Why?" asked Joshua.

"It would tell me if the environment is beginning to warm up. It would tell me if the jet stream patterns are changing."

"What kind of stream?" Joshua asked.

"The jet stream," explained Dr. Key, "is the river of air that moves storms over the Earth. If I could build a flying machine to take atmospheric readings, I could determine if the rising levels of CO_2 are affecting temperatures and air pressure. I'll need two jet engines, a large thermometer, a couple of electronic cameras and various other spare parts. Can you find them for me?"

Joshua's eyes got bigger. "This is 1961, doctor. I can find the thermometer for you, but jet engines are pretty hard to come by, and most cameras still use film instead of electronics. I guess I can check with my friends at the Air Force."

And with that, the butler dashed out of the lab.

Dr. Key walked through a passageway to the outside and took in the view. He loved the tall mountains on the island of Hawaii and the blue ocean that surrounded it. In fact, he loved all nature and wanted to protect it. Even more, he wanted to protect the people on the planet. That's why the doctor had studied the work of other scientists from as far back as the 19th century who believed that too much carbon dioxide in the atmosphere could actually change the climate of Earth. Now, Dr. Key suspected that CO_2 from factories, power plants and automobiles might be polluting the atmosphere, possibly causing temperatures all around the world to gradually warm.

"That's what greenhouse gases do," he whispered to the scenery around him. "They hold heat close to Earth instead of allowing it to escape into space. But I must find a way to prove if my theories on climate change are correct."

A few days later, Joshua returned with a load of Air Force surplus parts and spread them out before Dr. Key. "Ah, these will do nicely, Joshua!" beamed Dr. Key as he went to work sorting through the heap of components and wires. He picked up the thermometer. As he carefully studied it, an idea began to hatch in the doctor's brain. Gradually the idea turned into a plan, and the plan into a project.

Working diligently, Dr. Key attached two jet engines onto the back of the thermometer. "Now we'll have a flying machine!" he said excitedly. "But we'll also need some exhaust pipes." Finding four long pieces of metal tubing, he hooked two to either side of the thermometer like arms, and the other two below the thermometer like legs.

"Now, where are those two electronic cameras?" Dr. Key asked. Joshua retrieved the cameras from the pile of parts and handed them to Dr. Key, who fastened them near the top of the thermometer. When they were in place, they had the strange appearance of two blank eyes staring back at the doctor and his assistant.

"Your flying machine almost looks like a little mechanical man!" laughed Joshua. Dr. Key also chuckled at the resemblance to the robot toys he had played with as a child.

"Well, let's get it to the storage shed," said the doctor. "It's going to rain tonight, and we need to make sure our machine stays dry."

As night fell, the two men lifted the converted thermometer and carried it into a small shed behind the lab. In the fading light, they packed it securely away, and then the doctor glanced at his watch and yawned. "It's been a good day, Joshua, but now it's late. We'll need to continue working on this gadget tomorrow. Good night for now."

Joshua took the cue. "Good night, sir," he said, and made his exit.

Dr. Key's eyes were heavy as he walked back into his laboratory. As he sat down in his comfy desk chair, he admitted to himself that this job was going to be more work than he had planned. He closed his weary eyes and was soon fast asleep.

At daybreak, Joshua awakened Dr. Key with a cup of steaming hot tea. "Oh, thank you Joshua," said the doctor, putting the cup to his lips and taking a sip.

"That was quite a storm last night," said the butler. "Did the thunder and wind keep you awake? There was one crash of thunder that was particularly close."

"I must have slept right through it," answered the doctor. Then he suddenly sat upright. "My flying machine! Let's hope the storm didn't damage the storage shed!"

The two ran outside. What they saw made their hearts sink. An ugly black streak ran the length of the small building's roof to a hole in its top. "Lightning!" the two men shouted together in dismay.

They pulled open the door to the shed and looked inside. Yes, lightning had pierced the shed's roof, but all of the building's contents appeared to be undamaged. Relieved, they turned to go, but a sudden noise in the corner made them whirl around.

The two men gasped. A few feet away, a small metal creature sat up and blinked at them. "What is it?" asked Joshua, his voice shaking.

Instantly Dr. Key recognized the thermometer, the jet engines and the cameras from the Air Force surplus that Joshua had collected. He and Joshua stared in disbelief at the machine, apparently brought to life by the lightning bolt's electrical charge.

"It's alive!" whooped Dr. Key.

Joshua nearly fainted. Holding onto Dr. Key for support, he and the doctor tiptoed over to the curious creature and stretched out a hand to it. The machine, cooing softly like an infant, lifted its hand to meet the doctor's.

"I must be dreaming," said Joshua, having difficulty with his words. "It's… it's a living baby thermo…thermometer!"

"That's it!" said Dr. Key excitedly. "Thermo! We will give him the name Thermo! Thermo the Flying Thermometer!"

Thermo was indeed a baby. His first few months of life were marked by sleepless nights and tantrums. Gradually, Thermo learned to crawl, and then to walk, and Dr. Key soon discovered he could program English into the little thermometer's memory banks

One day Thermo looked at Dr. Key, pointed upwards, and said his first word. "Sky," he murmured.

"Did you hear that, Joshua?" marveled Dr. Key. "It's time to teach Thermo to fly!"

Dr. Key took Thermo outside to a platform he had built with a safety net under it. Thermo seemed to know what it all meant, and gave a quick blast of delight from his jet engines, lifting the young thermometer a few feet into the air. Dr. Key and Joshua clapped their hands.

"That's it, Thermo! That's how you fly!" they said.

Thermo giggled as he let loose a few more jet blasts, lifting him higher, and then moving him from side to side. But suddenly the jets went cold, and Thermo plunged to the ground, landing with a crash. That's when Thermo uttered his second word.

"Ow!"

"That's enough for one day," laughed Dr. Key. "We'll try again tomorrow."

As the weeks and months went by, Thermo eventually mastered the art of flying, and soon he was not only shooting up to higher altitudes, he was turning somersaults and cartwheels in the sky over Mauna Loa. As Dr. Key watched his creation play, he imagined Thermo exploring the skies over the Arctic and Antarctic and gathering valuable temperature data above tropical oceans and glaciers.

"Someday," said Dr. Key, "this little thermometer is going to help save the world."

Thermo heard him. "Don't call me little!" he shouted.

In the real world, Dr. Charles David Keeling inspired the character of Dr. Emanuel Key, who established his laboratory on Mauna Loa, Hawaii in 1958. Dr. Keeling was the renowned climatologist who came up with the "Keeling Curve," showing that levels of carbon dioxide were rising due to the burning of fossil fuels. CO_2 measurements continue to be taken at the observatory on Mauna Loa.

WORLD OF THERMO: THERMOMETER RISING 7

Story 2: Playing with the Clouds

It was a beautiful bright mid-summer's day in the Great Plains of the United States. It was now the mid-1960s, and Thermo the Flying Thermometer was having a grand time playing with his cloud pals Puffy and Fluffy. Dr. Key had given Thermo permission to begin exploring the world.

"How do you fly through the air without engines?" Thermo asked his friends as he fired up his jets to stay aloft.

"We're clouds!" shouted Puffy and his sister Fluffy together.

"We're made of tiny water droplets," said Fluffy.

"That's right," said Puffy. "Humans call us fair weather cumulus clouds."

"Wow," said Thermo, "you must not weigh very much if you can simply float in the air."

"To tell the truth, we each weigh about as much as a hundred elephants," Fluffy said.

"What?" cried Thermo in disbelief. "If you weigh so much, how do you float?"

Puffy and Fluffy smiled at each other. "It's really very simple," Fluffy said. "Our water droplets are so tiny that the rising motion of the air keeps them suspended in the sky."

"In fact," added Puffy, putting on his best school teacher voice, "the air around us is actually heavier than we are, so we can climb very high." And with that, he and Fluffy hitched a ride on an air current and darted away. "Follow us, Thermo!" called Puffy, and off they went.

After floating over the Plains for a few miles, young Thermo looked up and saw Wispy, a handsome but delicate cloud with white curls. "Who are you?" asked Thermo.

"I'm Wispy," the curly cloud answered.

"You don't look like my friends Puffy and Fluffy," said Thermo. "You're much thinner, and so high!"

"About thirty thousand feet high," bragged Wispy. "I'm a cirrus cloud." Then turning his attention to Puffy and Fluffy below, he taunted them. "Hey little clouds, I bet you can't fly this high!"

Puffy, who never could turn down a dare, told Thermo and Fluffy, "I'll show that little wisp he has nothing on me!"

Alarmed, Fluffy yelled up to her brother, who was now flying even higher, "Come back down and just ignore that Wispy cloud!"

Thermo was also worried, but he didn't blame Puffy. He also hated it when anyone called him "little."

Ignoring his sister, Puffy began to rise ever higher. But suddenly, his mood began to change. He felt sadder and began to darken. He also grew bigger and bloated. As Fluffy and Thermo watched nervously, Puffy began to shed tears of rain.

"Oh no!" cried Thermo. "You are turning into those dark clouds we've often seen in the distance. What are they called?"

"Thunderstorms!" cried Fluffy. "Oh, please come down, Puffy!"

Wispy waited for the little cloud in anticipation, knowing exactly what was happening. Puffy was changing from a fair weather cumulus cloud into a cumulonimbus, a deep, tall, dark thunderstorm cloud. Soon, Puffy would become electrified, and lightning bolts would crash inside him, through him, and fly out from him.

Thermo was suddenly in action. With a quick blast from his jets, the little thermometer propelled himself high above his poor fattening friend. Then pointing his engines downward, he blew a warm wind onto Puffy from above. Immediately Puffy stopped rising.

Fluffy was surprised, but overjoyed. "Thermo! You made a cap over Puffy!"

"I did?" Thermo was even more surprised than Fluffy.

"Yes!" said Fluffy. "The cold air above was making Puffy rise higher and higher and turning him more angry and unstable. But the hot air from your jets put a cap of warm air on him, so he couldn't rise or grow anymore."

As the two watched, Puffy slowly shrank in size and rejoined his friends.

"Thanks Thermo," said Puffy. "You saved me from exploding into a severe thunderstorm."

Annoyed, Wispy watched from above. "Rats," he grumbled, "I was hoping to make more cirrus clouds like myself at the top of that storm. Guess I'll have to try my tricks somewhere else."

And with that, Wispy caught a jet stream wind current and was gone.

In the real world, the weight of the average cumulus cloud is just over one million pounds. Its weight is spread out into millions of tiny water droplets, and rising air currents keep the droplets floating in the air. Cumulus clouds can easily blossom into thunderstorms, provided there is enough moisture and upward motion in the atmosphere. A "cap" is caused by a layer of warm air above that prevents more air from rising and forming thunderstorms, even when there is plenty of moisture to fuel them. When thunderstorms do form, anvil-shaped formations made of cirrus clouds develop at the top of the storms. When the storms dissipate, those cirrus clouds are often all that remain.

Story 3: Carbo's Release

Deep within a dark and enormous cave, Carbo the Carbon Molecule slept peacefully, just as he had been doing for the last sixty million years. Before that, Carbo had been very much awake. As part of a prehistoric fern, he had led an active life until a large dinosaur, a Triceratops, ate the fern and trapped him inside the beast's stomach.

Shortly after that, the Triceratops died, but Carbo lived on, even as the dinosaur and the carbon-filled plants inside it decomposed and became part of the soil. In time, Carbo found himself buried deep in the ground, along with millions of his friends inside other decaying plants. Over the centuries, Carbo became part of a huge group of other carbon atoms, all taking a sixty-million-year-long nap in a coal deposit.

Six hundred thousand centuries is a long time to sleep, and when in the 19th century Carbo was finally jostled out of his long slumber, he was not quick to awaken fully.

"Wh-what was that?" he mumbled. He sensed movement, but couldn't see anything in the dark. "I must be having a bad dream." He closed his eyes and turned over as sleep overtook him again.

Carbo didn't realize that what had nudged him from his dreams was a coal miner. The year was 1870 and the miner had dug him out of his cave along with many of his friends. Carbo's peaceful nap was about to end.

Several days later he awoke again, this time with a start. A sharp hot pain brought him suddenly and rudely out of his dreams. "Where am I?" Carbo asked as he looked around. He felt a constant jostling and a rhythmic clatter somewhere beneath him. He was inside a hot metallic enclosure, but through cracks in the metal he could see fields and trees and shrubs zipping by. Carbo was being burned in the engine of a locomotive heading across the U.S. prairie, moving westward toward the Rockies.

Suddenly Carbo felt himself rise into the air, up through some sort of tunnel, and then emerged into a bright blue sky. The burning sensation was immediately gone, and he felt a sense of freedom and euphoria.

"I am released!" Carbo shouted at the top of his microscopic lungs. Tumbling head over heels and circulating through the air with other fellow carbon dioxide molecules, he suddenly felt purposeful. He was helping to warm good old planet Earth.

"Yes!" Carbo declared. "This is my job! This is what I will live for."

If powerful microscopes had existed in the 1800s, humans might have been able to see Carbo's appearance, which resembled one large ball with two slightly smaller balls attached to it. The larger ball was an atom of carbon, and the smaller ones were oxygen atoms, thus his nickname, CO_2. Carbo's face was ghastly, with dark piercing eyes and a mouth filled with crooked teeth.

Having been trapped for sixty million years, Carbo understood that if he wanted to remain free, he would need to stay in the air and out of the way of plants and trees. He knew from experience that they would breathe him in and trap him again if they could. He never forgot how long ago, during the Cretaceous period of Earth, the fern had trapped him. Later, that fern was lunch for the Triceratops.

It's a good thing that plants couldn't read Carbo's mind. If they could, they would hear him say, "I don't like you, plants. You trap carbon and breathe out oxygen. You are my enemy."

As Carbo spent his first decades of freedom roaming the late 19th century atmosphere, he noticed that more and more of his brethren were being released by those silly humans who insisted on digging up coal and then burning the stuff. He also discovered that not all carbon dioxide molecules were alike. Like him, only the prehistoric carbon molecules released into the air had any feelings or intelligence at all. For some reason, carbon that was already part of the air before the Industrial Age, that is, before humans started burning coal, simply had no life.

Carbo didn't think too much about that. Nor did he think much about humans either, other than the fact that he was quite thankful for them. Only they could find the coal deposits and continue to release his friends. So now and then, Carbo breezed around their human heads whispering encouragement to them, hoping he could help them find more coal deposits and thus release more molecules like him.

"Think of all the friends I could lead," he said to himself, "if only they were all released from their deep underground traps."

Carbo knew the number would be in the trillions.

In the real world, the burning of fossil fuels such as coal increases the levels of carbon dioxide in the atmosphere. Carbon dioxide molecules, by their nature, trap enough heat near the Earth so that the planet does not freeze and so life can exist. That's why scientists call carbon dioxide a greenhouse gas. There need to be enough carbon dioxide molecules in the atmosphere to keep the climate just right for life to exist on the Earth, but if there are too many, the climate of the planet begins to warm unnaturally. That is what is known as the "greenhouse effect."

Story 4: Twista and Twisto Start to Swirl

After their close encounter with Wispy, Thermo and his cloud friends Puffy and Fluffy decided they should be more cautious in their adventures. Even so, as they soared out over the Great Plains, Fluffy became curious about the strange cloud formations she saw in the distance.

"Look at those dark clouds up ahead," she said. "Let's go check them out."

Thermo looked worried. "Okay, but we'll need to be careful. I don't like the look of them. Even from here they seem big and angry. Remember Puffy, you almost turned into a thunderstorm before."

The threesome glided ahead for about a hundred miles, and then Thermo made a signal to halt. "Let's don't get any closer for now," he warned. "We don't want those big storms to see us."

After a few minutes of observation, the trio noticed that one of the storms appeared to be growing. As the base of the clouds darkened, the storm started to rotate.

"Look at that!" cried Puffy.

"We'd better leave," suggested Fluffy.

"Not yet," said Thermo. He watched in fascination as the storm became taller and more massive, rising higher than most of the others surrounding it. In a few more moments, what looked like a large finger began to spin under the storm. The finger became a big funnel and started to sprout an ominous set of eyes.

"What is it?" wailed Puffy. "I've never seen anything so creepy!"

The spinning funnel opened its eyes and immediately spotted Thermo, Fluffy and Puffy. The storm moved closer to them, but the three friends held their ground. Then, in a thunderous and low-pitched female voice the funnel bellowed, "My name is Twista. Why are you spying on the Clan of the Storms?"

Trying to keep his voice from shaking, Puffy replied, "We were just curious about some cloud formations in the distance."

Twista moved in closer. "You puny little clouds and you—you little weird, flying rectangle thing, leave us be, or I will swallow you up! I am a tornado, and I am Queen of the Storms."

Puffy and Fluffy began to back off, but Thermo stayed put, the zipper-like thermometer that ran from his stomach up to his throat turned a dark red. "Don't call me little!" he shouted at the tornado.

In a demonstration of her power, Twista kicked up a cloud of dust and debris, stinging Thermo's camera eyes and sending him into a coughing fit. "Yes, you are little, my wee one," she said. "Now be gone! My husband King Twisto will be along soon. He is not as merciful as I am. I only uproot trees, but he batters buildings for fun. He picks up cars and trucks and tosses them around like toys. He has even been known to harm some humans. You don't want to be around when King Twisto is in a bad mood!"

"Come on, Thermo!" pleaded Puffy, as he grabbed the reluctant thermometer and they all sped southward toward clearer skies.

Once they were far away from the line of storms, Fluffy spoke. "Let's hope we never see that Twista again!"

It was a hope that would not be fulfilled.

In the real world, a storm in which the base of the cloud begins to rotate is known as a supercell thunderstorm. Given the right conditions, some supercells can form tornadoes. Tornadoes are categorized by their strength on a scale from zero to five called the Enhanced Fujita Scale.

STORY 5: PHOON

As the years went by, Thermo began to venture out farther from his home, and often by himself. One August day in 1969 when he was eight years old and still very young for a thermometer, Thermo decided to buzz over the central coast of the Gulf of Mexico. He had been there before and had always admired its mostly sunny skies and gentle surf rolling up against the shoreline.

What he saw this time was far from that.

As Thermo looked down, he asked himself, "What is going on?" Ominous waves were crashing below, and a dark sky threatened above. Thermo turned up his jets and flew high into the atmosphere, way above the level where the Wispys live, and moved southward over the ocean. Looking down over the Gulf, he saw something he had never seen before. Below him was a huge, nearly circular cloud formation covering a good portion of the Gulf's waters. Bands of thunderstorms spiraling out from its center reminded him of the tentacles of an octopus. Right in the center was a huge round hole through the clouds that looked like it could be the octopus's eye.

All of a sudden a low booming voice thundered from the storm, "What are you, little machine? What have those puny humans created?"

Startled, Thermo stammered, "M-m-my name is Thermo. Dr. Key created me to explore the world for him." Then, gathering courage he added, "And who are you to call me little?"

The huge spiraling storm roared back, "This time around the humans have called me Camille. I call myself Phoon, both Lord and Lady of the Hurricanes. When I appear, death and destruction often follow. Now go away little machine! In a few hours, I will pound the mouth of the Mississippi River with a mighty blow."

Thermo, still frightened but trying not to show it, remembered his experience with Puffy and Wispy. He thought to himself, *Maybe I can use my engines to stir up the air over Phoon and turn this storm into nothing more than a fair weather cumulus cloud.* He rose above the swirling clouds and began to blow warm air across Phoon's top.

"Stop that this instant!" Phoon ordered, striking Thermo with a powerful blast of lightning. Thermo was unhurt, but the sudden burst temporarily cooled his jets and he began to fall from the sky toward Phoon's churning circulation. In an angry voice Phoon threatened, "That was just a taste of my power, little one! Don't ever try that again, or I will turn you into a ball of melted metal!"

Seconds before plunging into the giant hurricane's eye, Thermo collected his wits and managed to restart his engines. With sonic speed, he dashed up and away from the angry storm. As he did, Phoon shouted, "Run little flying thing! I am too strong for you!" Then with a chuckle, Phoon scornfully added, "Little do the humans know that Carbo will make me even stronger in the future!"

As he rocketed away, a dejected Thermo wondered "Who, or what in the world is Carbo?"

In the real world, Camille was one of the strongest hurricanes to hit the United States, slamming into the Gulf coast on August 17, 1969 near Waveland, Mississippi with winds reaching 175 mph. Hurricane Camille killed more than 250 people and caused over nine billion dollars in damage (adjusted for inflation). Camille was a category five hurricane, the top rank on the Saffir-Simpson Hurricane Wind Scale. Wind shear, which Thermo tried to create over the fictional Phoon, is the change in speed or direction of wind with height, and usually disrupts and weakens hurricanes.

Story 6: A Vacation in Canada

Thermo was despondent after his encounter with Phoon. "If only I had been able to do something," he moaned. Disheartened, the little thermometer caught up with his friends Fluffy and Puffy and related the whole sad story to them. For minutes afterward, the three friends simply sat in stunned silence.

Finally, Fluffy said, "Why don't we get away from here? Let's leave the Gulf Coast and head north where we have never been. We could do some sightseeing."

"That is an excellent idea," Puffy agreed. "I love Canada, and we've never been north of Hudson Bay. Let's see what there is to see there."

Thermo considered it and then said, "That sounds good to me." Then with a sly smile he added, "I really need to chill."

All three friends howled with laughter. They knew full well how cold it was in northern Canada.

The journey took several days, but the trio finally got as far north as Hudson Bay, a huge area of water in central Canada connected to the Arctic Ocean. It was late August, and Thermo was surprised at how cold the air was. After crossing the bay, the thermometer on his chest showed readings down in the teens Fahrenheit. He began to turn blue and started shivering, but kept moving. Fluffy and Puffy, who couldn't feel heat or cold and thus remained quite comfortable, were delighted at the change of scenery.

After playfully gliding over the northern portion of Hudson Bay, Fluffy noticed something odd happening under Puffy. With alarm she cried, "Puffy, there are white flakes of ice falling from you! What is going on?"

Wide-eyed, Puffy noticed that flakes were falling from Fluffy too. Frightened, Puffy asked, "Are we coming apart?"

Thermo laughed. "Guys, I think these flakes are called snow. Dr. Key tells me that it's very common for even small clouds like you to produce snow in the Arctic."

Puffy and Fluffy's shock quickly turned to glee, and they began to giddily spin to and fro over the dancing flakes wafting softly through the air.

Thermo was startled when one of the snow flurries grew larger and suddenly sprouted eyes, a nose and a mouth. With a fairy-like voice the snow crystal said to Thermo, "My name is Flake. Are these my parents?" pointing to Fluffy and Puffy.

Thermo wrinkled his nose as he thought about that for a second, and then answered, "Why yes, I suppose they are. This is Fluffy and Puffy, and they helped create you."

Puffy and Fluffy giggled at Flake, marveling at his six-sided beauty. Then as more Flakes swirled around them, they began to cut loose. Laughing, whirling and twirling, they zigzagged back and forth and up and down, playing games with the little Flakes and entertaining one another as Thermo watched with amusement.

As the hours drifted by, Thermo's enjoyment began to wane. Unlike Puffy and Fluffy, he was starting to shiver. After several more minutes Thermo said, "I hate to spoil your fun, but I need to warm up. Could we please head south back to the United States?"

Puffy and Fluffy reluctantly agreed, and saying a fond goodbye to Flake and his many brothers and sisters, the trio traveled southward toward warmer and more familiar climates.

In the real world, snow showers (or flurries as the lightest snowfalls are called) can fall from cumulus clouds over the Arctic even in the summer, and during the winter over most of the Northern Hemisphere. As long as the atmosphere has enough rising motion to create precipitation, snow flurries can form.

STORY 7: ACT ONE FOR CARBO

Carbo was having a great time with his fellow molecules. He roamed the Earth, making sure that more of his kind continually spilled into the atmosphere. It wasn't a hard job; in fact, by the year 1880 the humans were doing it for him, digging more coal mines and burning the dark and dusty rocks for fuel.

"It's so lovely to see you, and you and you and you," said Carbo to the many newly freed carbon dioxide molecules, as locomotives and furnaces released them all into the 19th century atmosphere. "How wonderful it is to see so many friends!"

Every day more of his carbon buddies appeared. And though the numbers were growing, Carbo wanted still more.

He knew just where to get them. Carbo had discovered that coal wasn't the only source of carbon dioxide molecules. The ground was full of another substance made from the remnants of prehistoric plants.

"Oil," he said out loud. "That black gold is a gold mine of both old and new carbon friends."

But how could he convince the humans to take it from the ground? Sure, there were already a few oil wells popping up here and there in the United States and around the world. But to see his friends released in substantial numbers from the ancient liquid, humans would have to be convinced that they could not live without it. That meant the invention of an oil-burning machine that everyone wanted, one that everyone needed, a machine that no one could live without.

What kind of invention would that be? Carbo thought, as he floated over a city street. Looking down, he spotted a man and woman climbing out of their horse-drawn carriage. Carbo smiled and said, "I think I just found my answer."

Over the next few years Carbo saw human inventors and engineers throughout the world race to build a horseless carriage that people could afford to use every day. The humans constructed various versions of internal combustion engines to power such an automobile. Some engines ran on hydrogen and others on electricity, but the fuel that finally caught on was the one Carbo was cheering for.

"Oil! Oil! Oil!" Carbo shouted throughout Europe, and sure enough, the German inventor Karl Benz began to build cars that ran on a substance refined from that sticky black bile from under the ground. "Go Karl! Go Karl!" Carbo cheered.

"Oil! Oil! Oil!" Carbo cheered over the United States. Soon, an American named Henry Ford began churning out affordable gasoline-powered autos, eventually producing one car every ten seconds. "Go Henry! Go Henry!" was Carbo's perpetual cheer over the U.S.

To convince the gullible humans to drill oil in greater quantities, Carbo turned to the great state of Texas to do his bidding. Right after the turn of the century, humans began to extract the slick coal-colored "tea" from the soil of the Lone Star State, and Carbo was off and running, adding another cheer to his growing list: "More Texas Tea! More Texas Tea!"

To keep the humans producing more cars and drilling more oil and releasing more of his carbon friends, Carbo thought of a technique he had seen some humans use with their horse-drawn carriages. In order to persuade a horse to move forward, a man or woman sometimes tied a carrot to a stick, dangling the tasty treat out in front of the animal so it would keep walking toward it. In the first half of the twentieth century Carbo practiced a similar system, using automobiles as the carrot and humans as the horse. As the standard of living of most humans rose, demand for cars increased too. Humans wanted more cars, bigger cars, and faster cars. To get them, they needed more oil wells, more drilling, and more releasing of Carbo's fellow molecules.

Where will it end? Carbo mused, hoping it never would.

In the real world, Karl Benz produced the first automobile available to the public in 1885. In 1908, Henry Ford began mass-producing the Model T, eventually delivering fifteen million cars by 1927 with a price tag of $250 apiece. In 1901, the Spindletop oil strike near Beaumont, Texas proved to be the most productive oil well in the world, producing 17 million barrels of oil its first year, and beginning an oil boom that soon made Texas the biggest oil producer in the entire country.

Story 8: Skates Pays a Visit to the South

It was early January in 1973 and Thermo the Flying Thermometer was making another journey across North America. He loved sailing over the snow-covered ground, the iced-over lakes and frozen waterfalls. It was a view he could not get any other time of year. While he soared over the white and sparkling wonderlands, Thermo monitored the broadcasts of the human weather forecasters with the radio receiver Dr. Key had installed inside him. From those transmissions, he knew the humans were expecting some snow and ice in the eastern part of the country, but from the alarming readings on his instruments, Thermo suspected the humans didn't have the full picture.

Those readings advised Thermo that freezing air was moving into the area east of the Appalachian Mountains. He also knew that very moist air was coming northward from the Gulf of Mexico. From previous broadcasts, Thermo had heard meteorologists in the mid-Atlantic and southern states call this phenomenon "the wedge." From what Thermo could tell, this wedge had the potential of producing a particularly bad ice storm across the Deep South.

Thermo turned on his jets and headed toward Atlanta, Georgia to investigate. Upon landing, he went straight to work taking more weather observations.

"Yikes!" he said out loud. "The temperature here is already down to 34 degrees Fahrenheit, a stiff wind is blowing from the northeast, and my internal dew point meter reads 27. This spells trouble." With those kinds of readings, Thermo felt that the human forecasters should at least consider the possibility of an ice storm. It sure looked like the making of one to him.

In truth, the state of meteorology wasn't that great in the 1970s. Weather computers could not yet calculate conditions down to a grid of just a few square miles. In addition, forecasters lacked vital information about air temperatures and moisture content through all levels of the atmosphere, something essential to predicting ice storms. Still, Thermo thought the humans could do better, and wished they would at least warn people of what might be coming.

What was coming was a creature that Thermo had only heard about, a beast that traveled through the coldest clouds, and had a reputation of viciously toying with humans during winter. The creature's name was Skates, and Thermo had a nervous feeling the monster was nearby. Thermo flew up into the clouds to see if he could spot any traces of Skates. What he saw made him shiver not only with cold, but also with dread.

"Oh no," sighed Thermo, "Skates has been here all right." Snow was already falling from Alabama to the Carolinas. But if what he had heard about Skates was true, the snow wasn't going to be the worst part. On a hunch, Thermo flew down to a slightly lower altitude and took a measurement.

"Oh my, the temperature is above freezing here," he noticed. "That means the snow falling from above will melt into raindrops in this warmer layer of air. If the air below me is freezing, the rain will turn to ice, and a lot of humans are going to be in trouble."

Thermo dropped down closer to the ground, taking temperature readings all along the way. He was almost to ground level before he noticed much change, and the change disturbed him.

"It is just as I feared! The temperature here is below freezing. That means the raindrops will freeze onto tree limbs and power lines and bridges and roads."

And that is what happened. As Thermo watched helplessly, the freezing rain became heavier through the night and into the following day. He heard the loud cracks of pine trees and saw the flickering of lights as thousands of homes lost power and went dark.

Finally the little thermometer shouted with frustration, "I've got to do something!" Thermo had a sickening feeling in the pit of his thermometer that he might possibly prove powerless, just as he did with Phoon. As he rose higher, he spied what he was looking for, and the sight made him cringe. Up ahead was a thin, blade-like, upside-down-pyramid-shaped diamond figure.

"Skates!" Thermo whispered, his voice shaking, not with fear this time, but with rage.

With an eerie grin on his cold hard face, Skates was busy feeding more water into the clouds. At first Skates was too occupied to notice Thermo, but the sound of the flying thermometer's jets gave him away.

Surprised, Skates whirled around and furiously growled in a low and sinister voice, "What are you doing way up here, you little flying machine?" Then his spine-chilling grin returned. "Why, you're shaped just like a little cake," he observed with a menacing chuckle. "Maybe you could use a little icing!" The monster advanced toward Thermo.

Thermo was too angry to be frightened. "Don't call me little!" he yelled, "and stop pouring freezing rain on the South or I will melt you with my jets, you…you horrible icicle!"

Skates was amused at the boldness of the young thermometer. He let loose a long low throaty laugh. "You funny boy! You have no idea what you are up against, half-pint! I'll cover you so thickly in ice that you'll never fly again!" Then the creature reached out to grab him.

Almost too late, Thermo saw that Skates meant business. The ice monster was bigger and more powerful than he. As Skates's icy tentacles started to enfold around him, Thermo turned his jets on full and made a narrow escape as fast as his engines could take him.

As he sped away, Thermo felt humiliated and helpless, resigned to the truth that nature's villains would succeed in their dirty work once again. Downcast, the wee warrior dreamed of a day when he might eventually make a difference in the lives of the poor humans.

Right now that day seemed light years away.

In the real world, the Great Ice Storm of 1973 across the South occurred January 7-8. One to four inches of ice accumulated, closing schools and leaving 300,000 people without power for up to a week. The storm was the result of a combination of Gulf moisture meeting up with cold air forced against the Appalachian Mountains, a meteorological phenomenon called "cold air damming," or as locals often call it, "the wedge." Of course, the storm was not produced by a malevolent ice creature, but was a natural event.

STORY 9: LET IT SNOW!

After his encounter with Skates, Thermo went to Puffy and Fluffy for consolation once more. As his two friends tried to cheer him up, Thermo asked, "Why are storms so destructive and harmful to everyone? And why am I not better at stopping them? Isn't that why Dr. Key created me? Surely he wants me to prevent danger and loss." Looking sorrowfully at Puffy and Fluffy he pleaded, "Doesn't he?"

Puffy thought for a moment and then said, "Maybe you have been going about this the wrong way. Your jet engines aren't powerful enough to stop a storm that has already formed. What if you used them to change the atmosphere before the storm even gets started?"

"That's right," Fluffy added. "Then instead of a destructive ice storm, the humans would get snow like we had that time in Canada. That wasn't dangerous; that was fun!"

Thermo considered this. "That sounds like a good idea, guys. The next time I meet up with Skates, I'll go for it!"

Thermo didn't have to wait long. The very next month Skates tried to strike the Deep South again. This time, his plan was to create an ice storm not only in north Georgia, but also throughout the entire state, as well as in central Alabama and in North and South Carolina.

As Thermo flew back and forth taking temperature readings, he was alarmed to find that conditions were developing similar to last time. "Not again!" he shouted in frustration. It was cold, but there was just enough warm air in between the cold layers in the atmosphere to help create freezing rain and ice. Not only that, but he noticed that more moisture from the Gulf of Mexico was beginning to spread northward over land. He knew Skates was trying to make a repeat performance.

Thermo didn't have a moment to lose. Before precipitation started to fall, he jetted northward, and using his engines, guided more cold air southward. It was a time-consuming task, and most of the day passed before he could tell that he had made any difference in the air mass across the South.

"Now let's take some temperatures!" he whooped. Keeping careful to stay hidden from Skates's sight, the flying thermometer measured the temperature at various altitudes exactly the way he had done a month before. But this time, the air temperature had reached the freezing mark all the way from the clouds down to the ground.

"That's how it's done!" Thermo cried victoriously.

From above, the ice monster Skates perched on a flat dark stratus cloud to watch his icy handiwork unfold. "That's it, that's it," he laughed menacingly, watching snowflakes spiraling downward from the cloud. "The precipitation starts as snow and falls toward the ground. Then it falls into a layer of warmer air and…" Skates abruptly became silent. "What?" he cried in pained surprise as he watched the still-frozen snowflakes continue to fall. "Why aren't they melting? What happened to my layer of warm air?" He watched in horror as the snowflakes continued their downward journey and gently settled onto the ground below. Everywhere he looked there was a thick layer of white, with not a patch of ice anywhere to be found.

"That meddlesome little thermometer!" Skates howled. "I'll bet he's behind all this!" Skates dropped to a lower altitude and scanned the ever-whitening landscape below, reluctantly admitting that Thermo had outsmarted him. In fiery fury he cried out, "That scoundrel! That little cheater!"

Skates, boiling mad, dropped to the ground and pounded it with his fist, roaring in heated rage. As he did, slush and melted snow splashed into the air. All of a sudden his hot anger turned to panic. He noticed what looked like sweat drops rolling down his increasingly damp face. Temperatures at ground level had already begun to warm above freezing, taking its toll on Skates's normally frigid exterior.

"I'm melting!" Skates screamed. In a flash he sped away, escaping northward before thawing any further, bound for his home in Iceland, and far away from where he could do any more harm to the southern United States.

Meanwhile Thermo had dashed off to get his friends. "Puffy! Fluffy! Come and see!" he called gleefully. "It's snow!"

As the skies cleared, Fluffy and Puffy followed Thermo to witness the shimmering scene on the ground. Everywhere they looked, human children were building snowmen, throwing snowballs and making snow angels. Fluffy laughed and pointed to a snowman wearing a striped scarf, a pot for a hat and a carrot for a nose. "Look at him!" she snickered. "He almost looks like a real man!"

Thermo jetted down for a closer look. Just then, the snowman turned his head up to Thermo and said, "Hello, my name is Snowy. Who are you?"

Surprised but charmed, Thermo answered, "I'm Thermo the Flying Thermometer."

"A thermometer!" Snowy cried. "Can you take my temperature? I'm starting to feel a little feverish."

"Sure," said Thermo, as he set himself to the task.

With alarm, Thermo saw that indeed Snowy's temperature was rising, along with the air temperature around them. It wouldn't be too many hours before Snowy would be little more than a puddle. Thermo changed the subject. "I'd like to meet the children who built you. What are their names?"

Snowy brightened. "That boy's name is Nicky. He's seven years old. His sister Sydney is eight. They love to have fun in the snow."

Snowy's words proved true. The rest of the afternoon, Thermo, Puffy, Fluffy, Sydney and Nicky played and laughed and threw snowballs at one another. It was the most fun Thermo had enjoyed in years. Adding to his joy was the knowledge that he had been victorious over one of the atmosphere's most heartless brutes.

Too soon, it was time to leave. As the children and the little clouds said their goodbyes, Thermo looked with sadness at Snowy's shiny and now wet face and suddenly had an idea. He shouted to his friends, "Fluffy! Puffy! I need a hand. Nicky and Sydney, let's talk."

Before long, Thermo, Puffy and Fluffy had rigged a homemade sleigh and had placed Snowy on it. "There will be no more melting for you!" exclaimed Thermo. "We are taking you north for the rest of the winter. Alaska has perfect weather for snowmen this time of year!"

Snowy's smile would have been from ear to ear if the children had remembered to give him some ears. But Thermo could tell he was pleased.

"Wait, we need more clouds!" shouted Puffy. "Fluffy and I aren't strong enough to pull the sleigh by ourselves."

"Coming right up," said Thermo. He gave a loud whistle, and then, before you could say "Rudolph," eight arctic fair weather clouds appeared and hitched themselves to the front of the sleigh.

Puffy smiled and asked with a wink, "Which ones are Dasher and Dancer?"

Thermo laughed. "Ready?" he yelled. "Let's go!"

As Fluffy and Puffy and Thermo shot into the sky beside their new snow friend towed by eight tiny clouds, Thermo felt happy. He knew that not only had he finally thwarted one of nature's cruelest villains, but he was now in the business of making others happy too.

In the real world, the snowstorm of February 9-10, 1973 was just one month after the infamous southern ice storm. The snowstorm produced up to 18 inches of snow in some spots from central and southern Alabama through central Georgia into the Carolinas.

Story 10: Arrhenius

As much as Carbo was encouraged by what he saw the humans doing with oil and automobiles in the late 1890s, he soon discovered that not every human was blind to the effects of excess carbon dioxide. Carbo got this information from an unlikely source: two recently released carbon dioxide molecules who called themselves Roasty and Toasty. Carbo tried to see them as friends and equals, but in fact they were more like minions. That's because the pair, like most of the trillions of carbon dioxide molecules that had been released in the atmosphere, could not think on Carbo's sophisticated level.

But in them Carbo saw a willingness to do his dirty work for him, spying on humans and helping them create more machinery fueled by oil and coal. Though blundering and unskilled in most areas, Toasty had the uncanny ability to read human minds, though admittedly, he didn't usually understand what he read. Roasty's only known abilities were following orders and darting quickly from one place to another, though he performed even those talents inconsistently.

One day while Carbo was relaxing and floating on a light breeze, Roasty abruptly rushed up to him.

"Toasty has some news," said Roasty, out of breath.

"What sort of news?" asked Carbo, looking down his nose at the wheezing molecule.

"Uh…big news," replied Roasty, not sure of what else to say.

"Okay, where is he?" Carbo asked, growing impatient.

"Where is who?" Roasty asked, confused.

"Toasty! Where is Toasty!" yelled Carbo, now growing irritable.

"Uh…yeah. Uh, I don't know. Do you want me to find him?" Roasty asked.

"That would be a good idea," replied Carbo with a sigh.

"Okay, I'll go look for him," Roasty said, and dashed away at near supersonic speed.

Carbo wondered whether it was a good idea to employ help from any of his molecule friends, let alone these two. *Surely*, he thought, *there must be others out there brighter than this.*

Just then, Roasty returned, dragging Toasty after him. "I found him! I found Toasty, Carbo!"

"Thank you, Roasty." Then turning to Toasty, Carbo asked, "What is this news you wanted to tell me?"

Toasty obviously had something he wanted to say but was having trouble putting it into words. "I know I need to tell you this, Carbo. I know it's important, but I'm not sure why. I think it's bad news, but I'm not sure. I think it's important that you know."

"That's right," added Roasty, nodding fast and vigorously. "It's important. Real important."

Carbo was trying to hold his exasperation in check. "Important that I know what?" he asked slowly and with great self-restraint.

Toasty explained, "I just got back from Sweden where I saw a scientist named Svante Arrhenius. He has been studying the universe. At least I think that's what it's called. Yes, that's it, the universe! Anyway, I read his mind."

"Yes, go on Toasty," prodded Carbo as if he were talking to a child. "I'm listening."

Toasty continued. "This scientist, this Svante what's-his-name, is interested in all the chemicals that make up the atmosphere. He even has a theory to explain ice ages, whatever those are."

Carbo's patience was running very thin. "And why is that so important to me?" he asked Toasty, his irritation beginning to surface once more.

"Because," began Toasty, taking a deep breath and then suddenly spilling his words out all at once, "he's calculating how changes in the levels of carbon dioxide in the atmosphere might raise the Earth's temperature through the greenhouse effect."

There was silence. Roasty, looking puzzled, stared at Toasty, having no idea of the meaning of what his companion had just said. Toasty continued to look at Carbo expectantly, waiting for a reaction. Several seconds passed, then Carbo spoke evenly.

"He knows about us?"

Toasty looked blank. "I guess so."

"And he knows about the greenhouse effect?"

"Uh…apparently," answered Toasty, not making the connection.

"So," Carbo said, articulating each word, "You're telling me that a climate scientist has discovered our strategy?"

Toasty was flustered. "Uh…yes. I mean, no. Uh…do we have a strategy?"

Roasty looked back and forth at Carbo and Toasty, totally befuddled "What's a strategy?" he asked.

Carbo sat deep in thought for a moment, darkness crossing his face. Then catching himself, he relaxed. "Not to worry. One lone human scientist isn't going to make a difference. No one will believe him. Relax guys, and have some oxygen soup. I made it fresh today."

Food was something Roasty and Toasty could understand. Carbo handed them each a molecule-sized bowl and the two dove in, slurping loudly.

Carbo sat back down, contemplating, wondering. Then he shook it off. "No, not to worry," he murmured.

But something told him not to be so sure.

In the real world, climate scientists praise and admire the early work of Svante August Arrhenius, a Swedish physicist and chemist. In 1896, as part of his development of a theory to explain the ice ages, Arrhenius is credited with calculating how increases in carbon dioxide in the atmosphere would increase Earth's temperature because of the greenhouse effect.

STORY 11: OUTBREAK

IT was a beautiful day in the spring of 1974, only about a year after Thermo's encounter with Skates, the dreadful ice monster. The little thermometer and his cloud pals Puffy and Fluffy were taking a leisurely flight toward the Ohio Valley in the eastern United States.

"This way!" Thermo directed, as he guided his cumulus friends across the Mississippi River.

"Right behind you!" shouted Puffy.

Up ahead, Thermo noticed a great wall of clouds stretching east of the mighty Mississippi. He watched, as the storm clouds rapidly grew taller and angrier. The last time Thermo had seen a sight like this was when he confronted Twista and her Clan of the Storms.

"I don't like the looks of that," fretted Fluffy, slowing down.

"Neither do I," said Thermo as he came to a halt. Examining the clouds' massive structure, he noticed the lines of storms were broken into smaller sections. They were boiling up higher and becoming more numerous. A flash of lightning illuminated one from the inside.

"What in the world is the Clan of the Storms up to?" questioned Thermo, scanning the sky for any sign of Twista.

As Puffy watched the spooky spectacle he answered, "I don't know, but it can't be good. What I do know is that we can't do much to stop it."

"True," agreed Thermo. Then he remembered that during his terrifying run-in with Twista she had mentioned her husband Twisto and how he enjoyed destroying buildings and harming humans. "I think Twisto might be coming," Thermo said uneasily.

Puffy was thinking the same thing. "I have an idea, Thermo. Is there a way you can warn at least one or two humans in advance of Twisto's attack? Perhaps they could get the word out to others. They have ways of broadcasting to one another, you know."

"Yes, television," offered Fluffy.

"And radio," added Puffy.

Thermo nodded. "And I've also heard that there's a new kind of radio system devoted entirely to weather information. It's called NOAA Weather Radio."

"That's right," said Puffy. "It sends out warning messages from the offices of the U.S. Weather Bureau."

"It's called the National Weather Service nowadays," Thermo informed. "Where's the closest city with a Weather Service office?"

Puffy scanned the horizon. "I'm not sure, but probably in that direction," he said, pointing toward Cincinnati, Ohio.

"Okay let's go!" shouted Thermo, and the three hurried off, eastbound.

On the way, Fluffy called out to Thermo, "How are you going to warn the Weather Service meteorologists without being seen?"

Thermo knew she was right. Dr. Key had given him strict orders to keep hidden from adult humans. "I don't know yet," answered Thermo. "We'll cross that bridge when we come to it."

Soon they arrived at a building with a giant antenna on the roof. "Here we are." said Thermo. "This is the office of the National Weather Service."

The three peeked inside a window and saw humans scurrying about. Some were examining crude printed maps from Teletype machines. Others were talking on telephones. Still others were glued to an electronic screen with a bright line sweeping around it like the second hand on a clock. Thermo had seen the same thing in Dr. Key's laboratory. It was a weather radar monitor. Several humans were hunched over it, glued to its image.

"Those are the people we need to warn!" Thermo called to his two friends. "See them, Puffy? Right there, Fluffy!" He looked around, but the two had inexplicably disappeared.

"Puffy! Fluffy!" called Thermo in alarm. "Where are you?"

"We're right here," answered Fluffy's voice. "We're right in front of you."

"I don't see you," said Thermo, confused.

"That's because we've evaporated," Puffy said. "Down here near the ground the warmer temperatures no longer allow condensation, so our cloud droplets have turned to water vapor."

"Of course!" Thermo realized. "Water vapor is an invisible gas!" A tiny light bulb suddenly illuminated inside Thermo's head.

"Puffy and Fluffy! You can warn the meteorologists without being seen! Just slip inside and whisper a warning in their ears. Tell them Twisto is on the way."

"That's a great idea, Thermo!" whooped Fluffy. "Let's go for it, brother!" And with that, the two clandestine clouds inconspicuously breezed inside.

Thermo watched through the window. He couldn't see them, but Fluffy and Puffy immediately headed for the weather radar operators. Leaning up close to the ear of one of the humans, Puffy whispered, "Look for Twisto!"

Fluffy flew to another and did the same. "Twisto is out there! Find him!"

Suddenly one of the meteorologists pointed at the screen. "Look, I think that's a hook echo!" The others bent to examine the blip on the monitor. Sure enough, the radar revealed the unmistakable curved image of a rotating thunderstorm.

"You're right," said another. "That storm could mean a tornado! Put out the warning over the Teletype and the Weather Radio system. This is going to be a bad day."

In fact, it was a bad two days, and the three friends witnessed it all. Thermo, Puffy and Fluffy flew back and forth from the Great Lakes to the South, watching helplessly as Twisto, his wife Twista and the entire Clan of the Storms freely and effortlessly destroyed homes, landscapes and even entire city blocks over thirteen states and part of Canada. They saw the tears of the humans as they mourned the loss of mothers, fathers, brothers, sisters and children. Thermo thought of Nicky and Sydney, the children he had met on that snowy day only months before. He could still picture their happy faces in his memory banks. He hoped they were all right.

When it was all over, Thermo and his cloud friends sat quietly, staring off into space, dazed at the destruction.

"I thought we warned them," said Fluffy, wiping away a raindrop tear.

"We did," sighed Puffy, his voice breaking, "and many humans heard the warnings and survived. But I guess that's just not enough sometimes."

They were silent for a few more minutes, and then Thermo said, "I need to go home. I need to talk to Dr. Key. Maybe he can explain why this happened. Maybe he can tell me what to do. Maybe he can make me…" He paused and then continued softly, "not so little."

Puffy and Fluffy hugged Thermo until he was damp. Then the three friends parted, promising they would one day meet again. Thermo sincerely hoped that would be a happier day than this one.

With a wave of his hand, the little thermometer turned his jets on high and rocketed westward, bound for the Hawaiian Islands and a reunion with his maker and guide.

In the real world, the April 3rd and 4th 1974 outbreak of tornadoes was called the "Super Outbreak," and was one of the worst in the history of the United States, producing 148 tornadoes, many with long tracks over dozens of miles.

STORY 12: A STERN LECTURE

W elcome home, Thermo!" shouted Dr. Key as Thermo set down on his landing pad at Mauna Loa.

"Hello Dr. Key! It's good to be home."

"Look at you, my boy!" observed Dr. Key. "My, I have missed you! I can't wait to hear all about your travels. Come in and have a nice cup of jet fuel."

Thermo had forgotten how much he missed the cave's ornate furnishings, the thick carpets and the colorful paintings on the walls. The familiar surroundings improved his spirits immediately, something he desperately needed after witnessing the ghastly destruction from Twisto across the Midwestern United States. As he sank deep down into a soft comfortable chair, Joshua the butler set a steaming cup of jet fuel on the table beside him.

"Thank you, Joshua," Dr. Key said to his helper, then turned to Thermo.

"It has been almost ten years, Thermo," he began. "You must have explored countless countries by now. I am looking forward to reading your data and memory banks to see where you've been. Now, tell me all about it."

Thermo told the doctor everything—his adventures with Puffy and Fluffy and their meeting with Wispy, his encounters with Twista and Phoon and how he was able to thwart the plans of the ice monster Skates. Dr. Key listened, first with smiles of approval and even a few laughs. But as Thermo continued his tale, Dr. Key's smile turned to a look of concern, and finally a disapproving frown.

Then, when Thermo finished up with his story about Twisto's annihilation of cities and the countryside during April's Super Outbreak, Dr. Key had had enough.

"Thermo, I am disappointed in you. Your job was to conduct research, not to play."

"Play?" asked Thermo, dumbfounded. "It didn't seem like playing to me. Didn't you want me to explore the atmosphere?"

"Yes I did," said Dr. Key, "and I'm glad you have been doing that. But I also wanted you to observe what humans have been up to, not interfere. Have you been paying attention? Only a few years ago, men traveled to the moon and back. Humans are making major strides in science, and all you've done is surf the jet stream playing with clouds and trying to be a hero battling forces that you will never overcome."

Dr. Key's words stung. "I-I'm sorry," Thermo stammered. "I thought you wanted me to stay out of sight from the adults. I only talked to children," he said, thinking of Nicky and Sydney once again. He smiled, remembering the snowball fight with them last winter.

"You can observe without getting in the way," admonished Dr. Key. "Now, no more excuses. You are small in size, but you are nearly thirteen years old and it's time for you to take some adult responsibility. You have already learned that nature can be cruel, but it is still nature, the way it was created to be. Natural things consume other natural things to sustain life. We eat other animals and plants to nourish us. Even plants must consume something; they take in carbon dioxide from the atmosphere, soak up the sun's rays and acquire nutrients from the soil, all in order to stay alive and grow. It's all part of nature's balance."

Thermo listened intently as Dr. Key continued. "Nature can be brutal. You know that from your encounters with Skates and Phoon and Twisto. Sometimes humans get hurt."

"Do you think Skates and Phoon and Twisto wanted to hurt all those humans?" Thermo asked.

"Perhaps," acknowledged Dr. Key. "But remember, if it were not for thunderstorms producing rain, there wouldn't be water to drink or grow crops. As destructive as Camille was, some parts of the country depend on the rain that Phoon provides. Ice locks moisture into the soil during winter. Snow often covers our food crops to protect them from dying."

"And so we can build snowmen," Thermo added.

"That's true, Thermo, but what I am saying is that some things in this world are natural and good and other things are unnatural and evil. It is very possible that something unnatural in the atmosphere is turning what is natural against us. If we can fight against what is unnatural, we can make our lives on this planet better. So far, you have done a poor job of that."

Thermo looked down, dejected. "I have a lot to learn, don't I, Dr. Key?" he admitted.

Dr. Key smiled. "Chin up, my boy. You'll get there. Now, I have a mission, one that I believe you are ready for."

Thermo brightened. "What do you want me to do, Dr. Key? Just name it!"

The doctor was suddenly serious again. "As I say, I believe that nature has been in a delicate balance across the planet since well before the dawn of civilization. In my scientific studies from here on Mauna Loa I have noticed something unnatural that is upsetting that balance. The level of carbon dioxide has been steadily increasing. I have reason to believe that this is due to mankind's industrialization of the Earth. The increase in carbon dioxide is leading to what we call a 'greenhouse effect' that could eventually be detrimental to life on this planet. I will grant you that it is simply a theory at this point, but that is what my research indicates. I need other scientists to join me in my studies. I won't be around forever, but this problem will be, if I can't convince anyone else that it is real. And that's where you come in."

"Me?" asked Thermo, bewildered. "What can I do?"

"I need you to do something useful. Stop wasting your time trying to fight nature, and instead work with it to maintain its balance. I know you have already used your thermometer on a few occasions, but I am asking you to put it to use with a specific purpose. Would you be willing to travel the Earth and record your temperature readings? It may seem like a small job, but I assure you, it is not. I have a hunch this planet will be warming in some strange ways, and it's time for us to act. Will you help me, Son?"

It was the first time since Thermo had been home that Dr. Key had called him "Son." It felt good.

Thermo perked up, "Yes, Dr. Key…I mean, Father. I don't quite understand everything you've told me, but I will do my best."

"That's all I can ask," said Dr. Key. "Until now you've been on your own in your travels. But from now on, I'll be with you."

"You're coming too?" smiled Thermo.

"No," said Dr. Key, "but I will install a two-way radio inside you so we can talk at all times. And since your eyes are cameras, I will be able to see what you see and record it all into my computers for analysis. You will be a key player in this project."

For the first time in his life Thermo felt important. "Thank you, Father. I won't let you down."

"Good," beamed Dr. Key. "Now, how about a refill on that cup of jet fuel?"

Story 13: Gettin' Colder?

By the middle of the 20th century conditions were warming across Planet Earth. That was both good news and bad news for Carbo the Carbon Dioxide Molecule. On one hand, it meant more molecules like him were being released into the atmosphere. On the other hand, if it got too warm, then the humans would begin to take notice, and in fact some scientists were already beginning to see the trend and suspect the cause.

That's the last thing Carbo wanted.

In the 1930s a long-term drought had devastated the Southern Plains. Known as the Dust Bowl, the area saw farmlands ruined by the windy and dry conditions. Since then, the weather had cycled back to a pattern of fewer long-term catastrophes, with only occasional weather and climate disasters every few years. Still, Carbo had cause for concern.

He called to his minion molecules Toasty and Roasty. "Hey guys, I want to ask your opinion on something." Carbo didn't usually get an intelligent answer out of his two companions. After all, they had a combined I.Q. equal to the freezing temperature of water—in Celsius. But he thought he should at least try.

Roasty immediately rushed to Carbo's side with Toasty not too far behind him. "What is it, boss?" asked Roasty, eager to help.

"I want you to think about something for me," Carbo began.

Toasty and Roasty immediately looked worried. "Think?" they asked in unison.

Carbo continued, "What can we do so that humans will release more of our carbon friends without their being noticed? Once climate scientists see the warming trend our kind has started, I'm afraid that humans will turn toward different sources of energy for their power, and we can't have that."

"No, we can't have that," repeated Roasty. "No sir."

"No, that would be terrible," agreed Toasty, nodding vigorously. Then he thought for a moment and asked, "Uh, why can't we have that, boss?"

Carbo sighed. "Why? Because using different sources of power wouldn't release any more of our friends. Only the burning of coal and oil and gas will do that."

"Oh, yeah, right," Toasty said, not completely understanding.

Roasty had been deep in thought the previous few seconds, which was longer than normal for him. Then he said, "Uh, Carbo, I have a question."

Carbo, surprised that Roasty could articulate any sort of query, encouraged him, "Go on, Roasty. What is it?"

"Well," said Roasty slowly, thinking hard about each word, "If we put enough soot in the air, wouldn't that help block out the sun and cool things down?"

Carbo saw what Roasty was getting at. "Yes, it would. If the humans burn enough coal, the soot would actually block the sun just enough to keep temperatures from rising, and perhaps it might even get a little cooler."

Carbo suddenly turned to Toasty. "You can read minds, right?"

"I knew you were going to ask that," answered Toasty.

"Can you also plant thoughts into the minds of humans? I've done it a few times, but we need to step up our game. If you could convince humans to keep burning coal for electricity without using any filters on their smoke stacks, the air would become more polluted."

"They're doing that already, aren't they?" asked Toasty.

"Yes," answered Carbo, "but we need it to continue, and on a larger scale. Only then would it begin to bring air temperatures down. What do you say? Is that a plan?"

"It's a plan!" shouted Toasty and Roasty together.

"Good," said Carbo. "Let's get to work!"

The two minions fell over one another scampering away to their task, each with a distinct sense of purpose and an eagerness to please their wise leader.

Carbo, meanwhile, readied himself to spend the next few years welcoming countless new friends to the atmosphere.

In the real world, Earth experienced a slight cooling trend from around the end of World War II until the 1970s. This fooled some climatologists into believing that an ice age was imminent. All the while, unfiltered smoke stacks pumped more pollution into the air, blocking some of the sun's incoming radiation. Finally residents in places such as Los Angeles, California and Birmingham, England complained so loudly that engineers began using smoke stack scrubbers in their factories.

STORY 14: HEATIN' UP

Thermo spent much of the 1970s diligently working on the special project Dr. Key had asked of him. The little thermometer took temperature readings throughout the hillsides and plains of North America, in the tropical jungles and mountains of South America, on the beautiful beaches of the Mediterranean and in the deserts of Africa. From the equatorial oceans to both poles and back, he measured temperatures over every surface of the planet, and when he finished it all, he started over again. His job was a sightseer's dream come true, and not only did he enjoy the journey, he received constant encouragement from his maker, Dr. Key.

"You're doing a wonderful job, Thermo," praised Dr. Key over the transmitter that the good doctor had installed inside Thermo's head. The invention allowed Dr. Key to communicate with Thermo from his cave on Mauna Loa, no matter where Thermo was in the world.

One day, as Thermo was taking temperatures on the north coast of France for the 120th time, Dr. Key's voice sounded in his head. "Notice anything different this time, Thermo?"

"What do you mean, Father?" asked Thermo, as he recorded his reading.

"You've been tracking temperatures at that location long enough to realize that the numbers are gradually going up," the doctor pointed out.

"You're right," said Thermo, "and I have seen the same thing in many locations throughout the world. The temperatures I've recorded are sometimes a little higher and sometimes a little lower. But aside from a few cold winters, the overall trend has been upward."

That trend was paltry, however, compared to what he and Dr. Key found the summer of 1980. May of that year gave Thermo his hottest monthly readings so far in the heartland of the United States. "It's 100 degrees Fahrenheit here in Dallas, Texas. In May?" Thermo questioned whether the thermometer in his chest was working properly, but everything checked out.

From Texas to the Midwest, Thermo's readings were often in the triple digits. "It's a heat wave like I've never seen!" he told Dr. Key over his built-in microphone one day.

Dr. Key agreed. "Thermo, don't be surprised by what you see. Unless we do something, this heat could someday become a lot more common."

Thermo couldn't bear the thought of those kinds of searing hot temperatures becoming normal, but he soon discovered that his measurements were only part of the story. As he flew over farms and fields, he saw crops shriveling not only from the extreme heat, but also from a lack of rain. The devastation sometimes went as far as his camera eyes could see.

Thermo called Dr. Key through the two-way radio. "This is awful! What's the cause of all this?"

"You know those air pressure readings you've been taking?" Dr. Key asked.

"Yes, the barometer you installed in my circuits has shown the pressure to be very high," observed Thermo.

"High air pressure means that the air is sinking," explained Dr. Key. "As air sinks, it compresses."

"What do you mean, compresses?" Thermo asked.

"You know before I ride my bicycle around Mauna Loa I always pump up the tires?" Dr. Key quizzed.

"Yes," answered Thermo, but still not understanding.

Dr. Key continued. "When I push down on the bicycle pump, the air inside the pump compresses. Have you ever felt the pump while I'm using it?"

"Yes," answered Thermo. "It gets hot!"

"You're right," said Dr. Key. "That is exactly what is happening in the atmosphere. As air sinks and compresses over the Midwest and Southern Plains, temperatures in the area get hotter."

"And the sinking air prevents clouds from forming, so we don't get any rain either," Thermo deduced, now getting the connection.

"On the nose, Thermo!" said Dr. Key. "That's why the humidity readings on your hygrometer have been so low. The air is very dry."

Just then, a strange creature materialized not ten feet away from Thermo. It looked like a huge brown bag floating in the air. From the front it was wide and tall, almost like a parachute, but from the side, it was as thin as a bat's wing. The same color as the parched dusty fields below, the figure wasn't like any sort of cloud Thermo had ever seen. In fact, the sky was completely void of clouds. As Thermo watched, buzzards circled around the creature. Since Thermo was the only object besides the sun in the bright boiling sky, the brown stranger noticed the little thermometer right away.

"Hello. What are you?" she asked politely. "Are you a little toy airplane?"

"No, I'm Thermo. I'm a thermometer. And please don't call me little."

"Very pleased to meet you, Thermo, and you *are* little of course. I'm Heatia and I make heat waves and droughts. See those scorched and withered crops down there? I did that," Heatia proclaimed proudly.

"Well you should be ashamed of yourself," scolded Thermo. "The humans need those crops! Without them their children will grow hungry. They are my friends!" As he spoke, Thermo's thermometer turned an even brighter shade of red.

"I really don't care," said Heatia nonchalantly. "My friends are the buzzards, which feed off the fruits of my labor. The hotter and drier I can make it, the better it is for them, and the better I like it. So if you don't mind, I'd like for you to take a hike out of here please. I'm planning on being around a long time, thanks to my new friend Carbo."

"Carbo?" Thermo repeated. Where had he heard that name before? Then he remembered; Phoon had said the name too. So, who was Carbo and what did Phoon and Heatia have to do with him, or her, or it? Those were the questions that filled Thermo's mind as he jetted away.

By August, the entire United States was baking under the heat wave. Across Texas, Oklahoma and even Kansas, Thermo measured temperatures that crept up near 120 degrees F. In the southeastern U.S. Thermo took a reading of 105 degrees in Atlanta. *When will it end?* he wondered.

What Thermo didn't know is that another creature under Carbo's influence was preparing to unleash another kind of fury. Phoon, empowered by Carbo's extra heat-producing energy, was building a strong hurricane named Allen in the western Caribbean. By the time Allen reached the Yucatan Peninsula of Mexico, Phoon had increased Allen's winds to as high as 190 miles per hour.

Thermo radioed to Dr. Key back in Hawaii. "We have a serious situation developing here. But I have a plan, and I hope you'll allow me to carry it out."

"Tell me, Son," replied Dr. Key. "Maybe I will."

Thermo related his idea to Dr. Key. When he was through with the explanation, Dr. Key said, "I think it's a good plan, Thermo. Just be careful."

"I will," Thermo assured him, and went to work.

Thermo soared through the sky until he reached the southern Gulf of Mexico. There, on purpose, he flew casually by Phoon's one big eye, jeering, "Hey there, you big old wet rag! Bet you can't catch me!"

"We'll see about that, you little wimp," boomed the hurricane, and though Thermo bristled at being called "little," he was happy to see that Phoon took the bait. The gigantic storm gave chase, though being of incredible size, its pace was slow. Not for Thermo, though. He buzzed around Phoon's tall columns of thunderstorms, and even flew in and out of its eye a couple of times.

"Oh, what big eyes you have!" taunted Thermo. "Oh, I mean eye. Singular!"

This only angered Phoon all the more, and the hurricane chased Thermo westward into the Bay of Campeche and toward Texas. Soon, Phoon was lashing out at south Texas, and in doing so, beginning to break down Heatia's dome of high air pressure.

Heatia was startled at the dramatic change of weather but wasn't giving up easily. The heat monster fought back with her dry air and managed to steer Phoon south of the Texas border. The battle raged on for more than a day, and when it was over, both sides had sustained injury. Heatia had weakened Phoon's power during its landfall in Mexico, and Phoon had seen to it that Heatia's days of producing drought and scorching temperatures were numbered.

When Thermo reported the outcome to Dr. Key, he was pleased. "Well done, boy! You are learning how the atmosphere works. Though you and I might have an influence in the character of the battle, nature determines the ultimate outcome."

Even as Dr. Key spoke, however, battles were brewing that could prove to be nearly insurmountable for both man and machine.

In the real world, 1980 saw two big weather events: the heat wave of 1980 and the monstrous Hurricane Allen in the Gulf of Mexico. One has to ask the question whether it was a coincidence that one of the worst heat waves since the 1930s met up that summer with one of the strongest hurricanes on record in the Gulf.

Story 15: A Presidential Brainwashing

Despite the billions of carbon dioxide molecules that humans had already released from burning coal and oil, there were not enough yet for Carbo.

"What can I do?" he asked to the air around him. "My carbon friends have been asleep long enough. I want them freed!"

Carbo didn't like the trends of the last few years. First there was the Arab oil embargo of 1973, making gasoline expensive for the United States.

"This is terrible!" said Carbo aloud, "The U.S. is the world's number one user of energy, and its people are buying less gasoline, not more!"

Then there was the suggestion from President Jimmy Carter that the humans should conserve energy.

"Conserve! I hate that word!" cried Carbo helplessly.

And then to make matters worse, President Carter put solar panels on top of the White House in Washington, D.C.

"Imagine! On the White House!" It was more than Carbo could stand. "I've got to put a stop to this!"

Carbo and his minions Toasty and Roasty had been manipulating human history since the late 1800s. Like Carbo, Toasty could read human minds and exert pressure on them, and both molecules had been fairly successful at convincing the humans to increase their use of coal and oil and gas. Roasty was a willing but less able partner in the effort, but his heart was in the right place. Now it was time for Carbo to up the ante.

"Toasty! Roasty!" Carbo called out to them. As usual, the eager Roasty arrived immediately, with Toasty trailing close behind.

"What is it, boss?" asked Roasty. "What can I do for you?"

"Actually it's Toasty that I need this time, though you can help," Carbo said, as the other companion made his appearance.

"Need me to read some more minds, boss?" Toasty asked.

"And I get to help!" Roasty boasted.

"I'm going to help you both this time," Carbo replied. "The United States needs a new President if we're ever going to get more of our carbon friends released from their fossil prison. We're taking a trip to Iran."

Toasty didn't ask why; he simply followed Carbo, with Roasty rushing to and fro, confusing activity with action, trying to figure out what the expedition might be about.

For more than a year, Iran had held 52 American diplomats hostage in the U.S. embassy in that country and President Carter had failed in his attempts to free them. But that was before the intervention of Carbo, Roasty and Toasty. The three were able to infiltrate the embassy, use their mind-messaging techniques on the captors and negotiators, and bring about the hostages' release, all on the very day that Carter's opponent Ronald Reagan was inaugurated as the new U.S. President.

"Wow, that was some elaborate timing," observed Toasty.

"Now, let's put the other pieces in place," directed Carbo. "First, the price of gasoline needs to come down."

"Done," said Toasty. "I've already put the thought into the price regulators' heads."

"Next," continued Carbo, "is the 55 mile per hour speed limit. Bring it back up."

"It's history," Toasty said. "No more energy conservation there."

"Now for the tough one," Carbo announced. "It's time to get the solar panels off the roof of the White House."

"Oh, can I help?" offered Roasty. "I'm good at moving things fast!"

"No need, Roasty," said Carbo. "The new President will do it for us."

Toasty hesitated. "Why do we need to do that, Carbo?" he asked. "Sure, it will help release a few more of our carbon friends, but not the numbers you're looking for."

"Oh, but it will, Toasty," Carbo corrected him. "It will send a message."

"Oh I love secret messages," said Roasty. "What's the message? Tell me, tell me. I can keep a secret!"

"It will be no secret," countered Carbo. "When the solar panels come down, it will be a signal to the entire world that the United States has no intention of moving away from fossil fuels. The U.S. is a leader."

This time, even Roasty began to understand. "And the world will follow the United States, right boss?"

"That's the idea, Roasty. That's the idea."

Even while Carbo, Toasty and Roasty were floating around the Oval Office of the White House placing their agenda into the new President's mind, Thermo and Dr. Key were back at Mauna Loa watching their temperature readings continue to escalate. Dr. Key looked at the data with apprehension and pondered, "What forces could be at work to keep humans going down this destructive path? Cui bono?"

"Cui what?" asked Thermo.

Dr. Key explained. "It's a Latin phrase that detectives and legal experts use when solving a crime. It means, 'Who benefits?'"

As Thermo and Dr. Key contemplated the question, the answer lay close, but just beyond their reach, in the increasing number of carbon dioxide molecules that were rapidly populating the atmosphere.

In the real world, these events during the terms of Presidents Carter and Reagan actually happened, though the suggestion that carbon dioxide molecules might have caused them is fiction.

STORY 16: TESTIMONY

By the mid and late 1980s, most climatologists were convinced that global warming was real, and that increasing levels of carbon dioxide in the atmosphere played a role. It was that growing realization that had Carbo the Carbon Dioxide Molecule worried.

"How can I get my carbon friends released if humans know about us?" he asked his minions Roasty and Toasty, though he didn't expect them to answer. If Carbo didn't have a solution, then his less intelligent companions certainly didn't. Even so, he continued thinking out loud. "Despite our best efforts," Carbo told them, "some humans are just too smart to be manipulated; and now, one of them will have his day in court."

It was true. Carbo had helped Heatia produce the lengthy and devastating heat wave of 1980 and was even now currently working with the creature on another project—a widespread drought throughout the United States. Yet it was that very drought that helped inspire NASA scientist Dr. Joseph Hastings to testify before a U.S. Congressional committee. When the day came for his appearance before the Senate panel, Carbo, Toasty and Roasty made sure they were there.

Carbo was concerned because he knew that Hastings, though not a formidable-looking human, had science on his side. As the middle-aged and slightly balding Midwesterner rose to speak, Carbo gave Toasty the signal. "Now!" he nodded.

While Roasty watched in typical slow-witted wonder, Carbo and his main minion flitted back and forth among the Senators on the panel, putting into motion their previously devised plan, probing the Senators' minds and making them grow drowsy and increasingly apathetic toward Dr. Hastings's testimony.

"What a comfortable chair you have," Carbo whispered to one of them, "perfect for napping."

"You were up late last night," Toasty whispered to another Senator. "It won't hurt to doze just a little."

Finally, as most of the representatives were nodding off, one of them, Senator Doubt, interrupted the scientist.

"Aren't you being a bit hasty about all this, Dr. Hastings?" he challenged. "Why, you yourself have said that we won't be in trouble for at least another thirty years and maybe longer. We may even have hundreds of years to fix this!"

Carbo smiled. That's what he liked to hear. He and Toasty picked up on the message and began to spread it to the others on the committee. "We really don't have to worry about this today," the two molecules convinced the senators. "Maybe we'll have the time and money later, but certainly not now. This is a conversation for the future."

As Carbo watched Dr. Hastings continue to make his case to a disinterested audience, the leader of the carbon molecules was pretty satisfied with himself. Just like centuries before when the emperor Nero had played his fiddle while Rome burned, Carbo and Toasty's soft whispers to the lethargic senators were like a violin's sweet lullaby, lulling them toward a false sense of security, even while their carbon friends multiplied in the atmosphere.

Meanwhile, the creature known as Heatia had come out of hiding and was taking advantage of the increasing number of carbon dioxide molecules, using them to help bake much of the country in blistering heat and devastating drought. Crops were failing, rivers were drying up and hundreds of humans were dying.

Thermo and Dr. Key watched all this from television monitors in the laboratory back in Mauna Loa. In shock and dismay, the doctor finally said, "Thermo, it's time to take action. You did it in 1980; you can do it again now."

Thermo appreciated the growing confidence his maker had in him, but this was going to require a different solution from last time. As he thought about it, an idea popped into his metal head. "Why don't I attract the Clan of the Storms to help break the drought?" he proposed. "This time we'll attack Heatia from the north instead of from the south."

"I don't know," Dr. Key said doubtfully. "Heatia's high air pressure has forced the jet stream far to the north, trapping Twista and her Clan in Canada." He thought for a moment and then conceded, "If you could stir up the Clan enough, you might force their storms to break free, move south, and rain on Heatia's little heat parade. It's certainly worth a try."

Now armed with Dr. Key's blessing, Thermo flew toward central Saskatchewan, where the Clan of the Storms was huddled and hunkered down with their leader Twista, unable to move past the powerful jet stream that kept them imprisoned in Canada. Spying them, Thermo radioed to Dr. Key, who was watching every move through Thermo's camera eyes. "Dr. Key, I'm in place. Here I go."

"Stay a safe distance away," Dr. Key warned, "but make sure they see you."

Then Thermo turned on his most derisive voice and shouted to the Clan, "Ha! Isn't it too bad that you Storms have to live in a cage! Don't you wish you could fly southward like me?" Then he stuck out his long red thermometer tongue at them and challenged, "Look how easily I can fly over the Great Lakes! Don't you wish you could too?"

Twista watched Thermo from her far northern perch with mounting anger. The other Storms in the Clan began to grow dark with rage. Finally Twista ordered, "Somebody get that little pip-squeak!"

As their tempers flared, the Storms began to jostle back and forth, trying to free themselves from their high-pressure prison. Twista was right in the middle of them all, pushing and slamming against the walls of the jet-stream jail cell. Soon, the cage began to buckle and weaken, until finally a tiny opening appeared. The hole was nearly imperceptible at first, but as more Storms pushed against the breach, it opened wider, until all of them finally spilled through it like a raging river, free to make chase.

Thermo stayed well ahead of the Storms. As he egged them on southward, the Storms moved over the Great Lakes and into the American heartland, their rain cooling and moistening the dry and thirsty land all the way. Twista, weakened from her ordeal, was not able to generate enough energy to produce her usual tornado.

"We can be grateful for that," Dr. Key observed, "and the clouds and raindrops are certainly a welcome sight. Heatia has had control of the area far too long."

As Thermo flew southward, he spotted Heatia making a retreat. But something else caught his ultra-sensitive camera eyes. It was a clear sphere with two other spheres connected to it. He had never seen such a creature before, but its twisted face told him that this must be the evil carbon molecule he had heard so much about.

"Carbo!" Thermo cried.

The creature stopped in its tracks and then slowly turned around. Recognizing the little thermometer for what he was, Carbo jeered, "Aha, you must be Dr. Key's little plaything. At last we meet! Yes, I am Carbo, the leader of the carbon dioxide molecules. Heatia and Phoon have told me all about you, and as you might expect, we are not pleased with your childish antics."

Before Carbo could continue his lecture, Twista's dark Storms moving out of Canada edged closer to them.

"We need to go, please," Heatia warned Carbo nervously. "I cannot occupy the same atmosphere with the Clan of the Storms."

Carbo was frustrated by this development, but couldn't argue with the heat monster. "We'll meet again, Thermo," Carbo promised. "And when we do, I won't be so inclined to back down. You'd best be on your guard, little one!"

As Thermo watched Carbo and Heatia make their retreat, he realized that he had found the very root of one of the biggest problems haunting the humans. Dr. Key, watching from the lab on Mauna Loa, knew it too.

"We have a tough road ahead of us, Thermo," the doctor said.

In the real world, Dr. James Hansen, a hero in the world of climate, inspired the character of Dr. Joseph Hastings. The drought of 1988-1989 was one of the events that helped trigger Dr. Hansen's testimony before Congress in 1988. The drought was broken only in late August of 1989, when the jet stream moved southward, allowing storms to produce widespread rain over the parched area.

Story 17: Kudzu

Carbo was furious. Not only had his latest drought deal with Heatia gone south, but since he had shown himself to Thermo, climate scientists in every nation surely would soon know of his existence. And not just his existence, but they would also know about all his released friends in the atmosphere.

I had no problem being thought of as a theory, Carbo mused. *But it's a different game now.* The war had escalated. The stakes were higher. The weapons had become deadlier.

Back at Mauna Loa, Dr. Emanuel Key also realized the battle had risen to a new level. As he monitored news broadcasts from around the world, he heard alarming reports of climate scientists being harassed and even physically attacked because of their views on carbon pollution. As he considered what to do, he realized that if anyone had the resources to counter this attack, he did.

"Thermo, I have another task for you," Dr. Key told his young creation. "Scientists in the field of climatology are in great peril, and I believe that lives are in danger. Many of them already know this, but I need you to spread the word. Can you do it without being seen?"

"I believe I can," Thermo assured his maker.

Armed with his father's life-saving message, Thermo flew from city to city and from country to country, delivering written letters from Dr. Key, warning climate scientists to be extra cautious. The letters pointed out that dark forces were at work to not only squelch climate science, but to silence the voices that spread its words.

At first, many scientists discounted the danger or simply hoped it would pass. That was until one infamous incident that forced them to reconsider the threat.

Thermo had only a few scientists left on his list of those to warn. As he jetted toward the home of one of them, he saw a tragic scene outside. An ambulance was parked in the driveway and two uniformed men were running inside. On the porch, a woman was weeping into her cupped hands. As he viewed the heartbreaking scene, Thermo heard a faint "whoosh" sound behind him. Turning, he caught a brief glimpse of a clear spherical creature speeding away. Thermo wasn't sure, but he thought he saw two smaller spheres attached to either side of the creature.

Once Thermo was back at Mauna Loa, Dr. Key read aloud to him the sad newspaper headline, "Scientist Dies from Carbon Dioxide Poisoning."

Thermo sat somberly next to the doctor, thinking. Finally he spoke. "Cui bono?"

"What?" asked Dr. Key.

"Who benefits?" Thermo repeated.

"Exactly!" Dr. Key concluded. "If I'm not mistaken, Carbo and his cohorts are behind this despicable deed."

"We need to tell everyone to beware of Carbo," Thermo said.

"In time, Son," answered the doctor. "I'm afraid people may not be ready to believe that living CO_2 molecules are the problem; Carbo and his henchmen have hidden themselves well."

After a moment of reflection, Dr. Key went on. "Thermo, you know that newspaper headline could have been about me, had I not had the protection of this secret cave."

Thermo thought about that. "Maybe we should find caves for other scientists too," he suggested. "They could live there with their families until the danger is over."

Dr. Key smiled. "Thermo, you are turning into a treasure trove of ideas. Go find us some caves!"

Over the next few weeks, Thermo scouted out a number of caves suitable for habitation. The only problem was that most could be spotted easily from the outside, and thus vulnerable to discovery by Carbo and his minions. As he flew over the Deep South, not far from the place that had been encased in ice by Skates years ago, Thermo marveled at the rapidly growing broadleaf weed spreading over the landscape. He set down near one of the plants for a closer examination.

As Thermo eyed the plant intently, it suddenly spoke. "Hello. I am part of the Vine of Life," the weed said, "but you can call me Kudzu. Who are you?"

Thermo introduced himself and then explained his mission, describing the desperate situation for climate scientists throughout the world. Kudzu grew more interested with every word. Finally the weed said, "I am the perfect camouflage for your caves! I grow fast, I grow tall, and during the day I take in the carbon dioxide that comes near me and release oxygen back into the air. If you plant me outside the door of every one of your caves, I will hide them and guard them from intruders."

And it worked. Hundreds of scientists moved into the caves that Thermo found and planted groves of Kudzu outside. One day, as Thermo was inspecting their handiwork, a large nearby Kudzu plant suddenly hiccupped. Thermo turned toward the plant questioningly.

"Excuse me," blushed Kudzu. "I just got a nose full of evil carbon dioxide molecules. But now," Kudzu said, exhaling loudly, "the carbon is my food and I breathe out nice friendly molecules of oxygen. Mission accomplished."

Soon, word got out among Carbo's released friends to steer clear of Kudzu, and the cave-dwelling climatologists continued their lives and their research, safe from the reach of Carbo and his minions.

"Foiled by a bunch of plants!" Carbo lamented.

It was back to the drawing board.

In the real world, carbon dioxide is not attacking anyone, let alone climate scientists. However, climate scientists and some environmentalists have been attacked, harassed and even killed because of their opinions. (See the Appendix for an example.)

Story 18: When the Volcano Blows

Carlos, stop kicking me in the head!" Juan yelled to his climbing mate. "I can't see! Hold that flashlight closer to the cliff so I won't stumble!"

The two men were slowly scaling down the caldera of the active volcano known as Pinatubo. They lived on the island of Luzon in the Philippines and were not far from home on a murderous mission. The mission was not their idea; forces beyond their control were dominating them.

Using a pulley support rope, Carlos said nothing as he slowly descended into the cavern in a zombie-like stupor, while Carbo's minion Toasty floated nearby. Since Carbo could be in only one place at a time, he had reluctantly begun to entrust Toasty with more authority. In turn, Toasty had brought along two new accomplices, Flame and Smother. Like Toasty, they both could read the minds of humans as well as place thoughts into their brains. But it was taxing work.

"You're losing control! You need to try harder!" Toasty coaxed his companions.

"I'm doing my best!" countered Smother.

"I'm already sweating!" yelled Flame.

It took every ounce of energy for these carbon dioxide molecules to force the hapless humans into doing their bidding. Now and then, Carlos and Juan had moments of lucidity when they suddenly realized that what they were doing would surely bring death and destruction to their villages and family near Mount Pinatubo.

"What are we doing, Juan?" asked Carlos in despair.

"I can't help myself!" was Juan's desperate cry.

Perspiring profusely, Flame and Smother concentrated all the more, guiding their captives back to their lethal assignment. Inside both men's heavy backpacks were parcels of powerful explosives, and the corrupt CO_2 molecules were determined they be put to good use.

Carbo had conjured up a plan earlier in 1991 to snooker the humans into believing that Planet Earth was cooling yet again. He hoped that would slow down the efforts of climate scientists trying to stop people from using fossil fuels for energy. Being a most intelligent carbon molecule, he determined that volcanic eruptions, if powerful enough, would temporarily cool the planet. Carbo's plan was now in motion, and he and his minion Roasty watched it unfold from a safe distance.

"Heatia will hate me for this," Carbo said.

"You told that brown beast what we were doing, boss?" asked the more-than-helpful but less-than-intelligent lackey.

"That I was going to cause a volcano to erupt? No, Roasty. The last thing that heat monster wants is for the Earth to cool."

It had taken months to find just the right volcano. Carbo had considered trying to reactivate the dormant volcano under Yellowstone Park in in the United States, but decided that such a blast would be too powerful. He wanted an eruption that would be strong enough to temporarily cool the planet, but not so strong that Earth would be sent into a mini ice age. If that were to happen, the resulting human annihilation would defeat his purpose, which was to convince as many humans as possible to burn coal and oil, releasing his carbon friends from their underground prisons.

Carbo's minion Roasty still wasn't exactly sure what his leader was up to. "So why did we have to find a couple of humans to help us?" he asked.

Carbo frowned. He hated admitting that anything was beyond his ability, but there was no other explanation. "We don't have hands to hold tools. We can't put timers on the explosives. But we can bend the will of humans to do it for us." He sneered, "They are our slaves."

Right now the slaves were being very reluctant. Juan was a strong young man, full of promise and energy. He was proving to be a formidable match for Smother, the carbon dioxide molecule in charge of manipulating him.

"Come on, Juan," Smother beckoned. "It's all for the best." Juan struggled against the will of Smother, but time and again, the molecule's mind-bending powers proved stronger.

Flame was having an equally challenging time wielding power over Carlos. "Show everyone how strong you are," tempted Flame. "Only a tough and muscular man like you could do something like this." Eventually, Carlos succumbed to the molecule's flattery.

After Juan and Carlos descended to the floor of the cave, they took the explosives out of their backpacks. Still struggling against their captors, they placed the devices into two crevices. They set the timers, and then began their climb back up the cliff toward the entrance. Flame and Smother planned to release the humans back into their village.

For a split second, Smother's curiosity got the better of him, and he gazed at the bubbling mud and magma at the base of the cave. "How deliciously deadly!" he observed.

In that instant, Juan wrestled his will away from his mind master, unleashed his tether, and fell bodily toward Smother. As he collided with the carbon dioxide molecule he cried, "I don't know what type of devil you are, but I'm going to take you down with me!" Surprised, stunned and exhausted from his mind-probing efforts, Smother fell toward the bubbling magma along with Juan.

Toasty and Flame watched helplessly as their companion and his charge dropped to their demise. Immediately livid, and knowing that the timers were already set, Toasty and Flame combined their energies to force Carlos to let go of his rope, and the other brave Filipino soul was gone as well.

The two remaining molecules rose out of the cave to safety, and minutes later, their dirty work was done. The explosives set off a series of earthquakes that would eventually lead to an eruption like the world had not seen in almost a century.

As Carbo watched from far away, he smiled. "Humans are good for something after all, Roasty. Now we'll see if this temporary reprieve from global warming will fool them."

Roasty just stared at the cloud of ash beginning to billow out from the top of the volcano.

In the real world, Mount Pinatubo erupted in 1991, sending ash clouds over the globe. This helped result in average temperatures throughout the world falling by about one degree Fahrenheit over the next year.

STORY 19: ANDREW

The summer of 1992 would be over soon, and there had not yet been a single tropical storm or hurricane to affect the United States. For much of the season, an atmospheric phenomenon called wind shear— brisk winds of different speeds and directions at different altitudes— kept tropical weather systems from developing over most of the Atlantic Ocean, Gulf of Mexico and Caribbean.

Not surprisingly, Phoon was getting restless. "I can't even drum up a decent storm these days," the hurricane-maker said in frustration. "Here it is already August and I haven't had a chance to upset a single human along the entire North American coastline."

Thermo had spent the summer flying over the United States taking temperature readings. He too noticed the lack of tropical activity in the Atlantic, but he also knew that a quiet start to a hurricane season didn't mean it would stay that way. In 1989 only one hurricane had impacted the United States before late September, but that was the month Hurricane Hugo had slammed into Charleston, South Carolina as the discouraged little thermometer watched from a distance, unable to help. Even now it still made him sad to think about the 86 humans who died three years earlier in that hurricane and the 100,000 left homeless by it. Thermo knew there was plenty of time for Phoon to raise its ugly head before the Atlantic hurricane season was over.

Finally in mid-August, Phoon saw an opportunity. "Aha!" it exclaimed, perking up. "The shearing winds are gone! Time for a little fun!"

At his television weather office in Miami, Florida, Steven Woods examined his data and maps closely. "If the wind shear dies down any more," he said to a colleague, "anything that pops up over the ocean will head right toward South Florida."

That was precisely what Phoon was thinking. And if this creator-of-hurricane-havoc had any say in the matter, humans would soon see a storm develop north and east of the Caribbean Sea. "All my pieces are coming together," boasted Phoon, watching the falling air pressure and the rising wind speed.

Thermo watched the scene unfold from his bird's eye view in the sky above. His internal barometer confirmed that Phoon's air pressure was dropping, and the anemometer Dr. Key had installed inside him measured increasing wind speeds. Thermo radioed Dr. Key in Mauna Loa, Hawaii and told him, "Phoon is getting stronger. I think there's going to be a hurricane soon. I have to do something."

"Thermo!" Dr. Key raised his voice. "You know that Phoon is too strong for you! Remember the last time you tried to stop it. Your fight against Camille almost cost you your life!"

"That time Phoon was already a major hurricane," Thermo argued. "If I can do something before this storm strengthens, I'll have a better chance."

Dr. Key was adamant. "I have told you before; it would be a losing battle. Concentrate on the task I have assigned you! Do your job, Son!" And with that, Dr. Key signed off.

Thermo was indignant. "How can he expect me to stand by and do nothing?" More than anything, Thermo did not want to see a repeat of what Hurricane Hugo had done three years before. "I at least have to try."

Even as Thermo spoke those determined words, Phoon had already strengthened into a tropical storm, an opportunity to take on an alter ego, a sort of split personality. "You can call me Andrew!" Phoon shouted to the sky. "Now let's see if the first storm of the season can make up for lost time!"

Thermo decided to try the same tactic he had used years before when Phoon had called itself Camille. "Here goes!" he cried, and turned his engines on high, buzzing over the Caribbean Ocean. Trying not to be seen, he poised his jets over Andrew and blew as much wind as he could muster across its top, trying to mimic the wind shear that had kept the storm from developing earlier.

Phoon felt the sudden change in wind direction and howled, "It's that little thermometer again! Will he never learn?" Looking up, Phoon spotted Thermo trying to blow the top off of the storm, a goal that he was, in fact, starting to accomplish.

Phoon clearly sensed the difference. Feeling more pressured and increasingly off balance, the tropical storm began to stumble. But Phoon was not about to give up. "I'll get you, you mechanical pest!" shouted Phoon-turned-Andrew.

With a giant cloud-band tentacle, Phoon swatted at Thermo, almost knocking him out of the sky. "Close!" Phoon shrieked. "But not close enough! Shall we try that again, little one?"

"Don't call me little!" Thermo screamed, and kept pumping hot air out of his jets.

Phoon took two more swipes at the jet-propelled thermometer, narrowly missing him before Thermo reluctantly decided he'd better get out of the storm's way. Thermo sighed to himself as he flew out of the tropical monster's reach, "I only hope my wind shear was enough to make a difference."

It wasn't. Almost as soon as Thermo was gone, the now livid Phoon began to gain strength, channeling all of its anger into building Andrew's energy.

Thermo glanced away from the scene as a rickety old aircraft lumbered toward Phoon's new personality. He expected to see Phoon lash out at it as well, but then remembered Dr. Key had once told him the Hurricane Hunter planes only took readings in a storm; they had no power to diminish it. *Maybe that's what Dr. Key is trying to tell me to do*, he considered.

At his South Florida TV station, Steven Woods was watching Andrew's growing wrath via radar images and photos from satellites looking down on the Atlantic. For a split second he caught a tiny thermometer-shaped blip on the screen. "A UFO?" he wondered out loud, but as quickly as it came, it was gone. Besides, Woods had bigger fish to fry. Andrew had strengthened to a hurricane.

"We are going to broadcast around the clock," he told his colleagues. "Even if it hits us, we're going to stay on the air."

Phoon's angry rampage swept over the Bahamas, its interaction with the islands weakening the hurricane a little. "Just a speed bump!" Phoon shouted triumphantly, and soon Andrew was stronger than ever. "Look out, South Florida!" Phoon bellowed. "You're next!"

As Phoon's fury swept into Florida, Thermo took refuge out of sight inside Steven Woods's television station. He watched as Woods maintained his vigil all night long, updating viewers on Andrew's progress, and advising them how to survive the hurricane. The non-stop coverage lasted a full 23 hours.

Thermo had felt defeat many times before, but this time, reality was genuinely sinking in. "I am little," he admitted to himself, "and nature is big. I tried to help, but I only made things worse." As he watched Steven Woods continue his tireless round-the-clock broadcasts, Thermo marveled, "Look at him. There is nothing he can do to stop Phoon, but he is doing his job the very best he can. And that's what makes him a hero."

At last, Thermo understood what Dr. Key had been saying all along.

In the real world, 1992's Hurricane Andrew was the costliest to strike the United States at the time. Raking Homestead Florida with 165 mph winds, Andrew made a second landfall in southern Louisiana with winds of 115 mph. Bryan Norcross, aka Steven Woods in our fictional story, monitored Andrew from its inception off the coast of Africa until it crashed into Florida on the 24th of August. At one point Norcross broadcasted an epic 23 hours non-stop to warn and advise South Florida residents.

STORY 20: STORM OF THE CENTURY

What do you make of it, Thermo?" asked Dr. Key via the two-way radio he had installed in his mechanical creation years ago. The communication system allowed the little jet-propelled thermometer to talk with his maker back in Mauna Loa while he explored the world, gathering data for Dr. Key's research.

"It's just as you said, sir," answered Thermo. "Temperatures here in Canada are very cold for early March. And there are signs that the cold is moving southward toward the United States."

It was now 1993, and Dr. Key was one of many scientists watching the potential for a powerful blizzard in the coming days. By now, Thermo had learned that he could not stop weather from occurring, but his work was valuable in not only forecasting what was to come, but also in bringing life-saving information to the humans in its path.

As Thermo turned to make another pass over Canada, he stopped dead in his tracks. Up ahead, a white sleigh, driven by eight lively cumulus clouds, was sailing across the sky.

"Snowy!" cried Thermo with joyful recognition. "I can't believe it's you!" He and his cloud friends Puffy and Fluffy had rescued Snowy from melting so many years ago. "What on earth are you doing here? The last I heard, you were headed to Alaska to live."

"It's absolutely marvelous to see you, Thermo," Snowy intoned. "I lived in Alaska for a season, but even that state gets warm in the summer. So I relocated to a more prosperous life farther north. I had to keep myself together, so to speak."

"Well you certainly look different from the last time I saw you," observed Thermo.

When the human children Nicky and Sydney had created him, Snowy had worn a pot on his head, a scarf around his neck and he had a carrot for a nose. Now he sported a black beard and red top hat. Even his sleigh was different. This one was made of clouds. And was it Thermo's imagination, or did this odd-looking cross-between-Frostythe-Snowman-and-Santa-Claus now act differently too? Even so, it was great to see his old friend again after all these years.

"Where are you going, Snowy?" asked Thermo.

"Ho, Ho, Ho, I'm going to help create a late-season blizzard for the American humans. I'm feeling rather spirited these days after that Philippine volcano cooled things down a bit, and I've brought along a trillion or so of my flake friends to help me out."

Snowy had changed; there was no doubt about it, and Thermo was confused. "How did you get the ability to create a blizzard, Snowy?"

"Oh that! Well, do you remember our friend Skates?"

Skates was definitely not a friend, but Thermo let it pass. "Yes, I remember him."

"Well, over the years he became sort of a mentor to me. He taught me everything he knows. I just gave it my own little twist."

Thermo didn't like the sound of that. After all, Skates was an ice monster that seemed to take pleasure in hurting humans. Surely Snowy hadn't become like that! Thermo wanted to know more, but Snowy's sleigh had already turned south and the eight cumulus clouds guiding it were obviously anxious to get going.

"Goodbye Thermo! See you around!" called Snowy.

"Snowy, wait!" cried Thermo, but then became silent. Dr. Key wouldn't want him to interfere. Even so, the little thermometer was worried.

Days later, back in Hawaii, Dr. Key and Thermo were glued to a television, watching weather coverage of what newscasters were now calling "The Storm of the Century." There was no arguing that it was a devastating event. Snowy had been a very bad snowman.

"I can't believe he would do something like this," said Thermo. "He was so nice before. That's why we saved him."

"Things change, Thermo," consoled Dr. Key, "some for better, some for worse."

This was definitely a change for the worse. The blizzard brought harm to humans in most of the eastern half of the United States. In addition to the snow and wind, Snowy had teamed up with the Clan of the Storms to produce tornadoes in Florida and even a storm surge of high water on the coast that would have made Phoon proud.

"Well," Thermo softly said to Dr. Key, "that's the last time I rescue a snowman."

Dr. Key's thoughts were a bit more philosophical. "Remember, Thermo, circumstances can be both good and bad, human actions can be both good and bad, but nature is neutral. As I've told you before, everything in nature has a purpose, but sometimes that purpose runs counter to human desires. Indeed, sometimes it runs counter to life itself. Snowy is part of nature. His kind has always been with us producing storms across the Earth. To him it's a game."

Dr. Key paused, and then said, "But I do agree that his heart has grown cold."

Thermo looked up at Dr. Key. "Did you just mean to make a pun?"

"Can't an old scientist have a little bit of fun?" Dr. Key smiled innocently.

Thermo and the doctor sat in silence for a full minute. Then Thermo sighed. "If nature is neutral, then what about Carbo and his henchmen? Are they neutral too?"

"There is natural carbon dioxide in our atmosphere of course," replied Dr. Key, "but our burning of fossil fuels created Carbo and his minions. They are different from natural CO_2 in the air. Even their molecular structure shows the difference. No, they are not neutral."

"So if humans made Carbo, perhaps he inherited some of their bad traits."

"Interesting point, Thermo," said Dr. Key. "You've learned a lot about nature, and about human nature too."

In the real world, the Storm of the Century (twentieth century) was also known as the 1993 Superstorm or the Great Blizzard of 1993. Central Alabama and Georgia received 6 to 8 inches of snow, and Birmingham received up to a foot, with isolated reports of 16 inches. Even the Florida Panhandle reported up to four inches of snow with hurricane-force wind gusts and record low air pressure readings. Between Louisiana and Cuba, hurricane-force winds produced high storm surges across northwestern Florida, which, along with scattered tornadoes, killed dozens of people. Record cold temperatures registered in the South and East in the wake of this storm. In the United States, the storm was responsible for the loss of power to over 10 million customers. In all, nearly 320 people perished.

Story 21: Tree Ring Circus

Don't slow down," Thermo urged his cumulus cloud friends Puffy and Fluffy. "I know it's hot and dry, but please try to hold out a little longer over the desert. We need to get these tree core specimens back to Dr. Cape before dark."

"I'll be all right," Fluffy panted optimistically. But in truth, the dry air was not only shrinking her size, it was sapping her strength. Her brother Puffy wasn't faring much better.

Dr. Key had asked Thermo and his friends to haul pine tree core samples from the White Mountains in Arizona to the nearby laboratory of Dr. Julius Cape. It was proving to be an arduous task.

"Why does Dr. Cape need these, Thermo?" wheezed Puffy, who was increasingly short of breath.

"He's a dendrochronologist."

"A dendro-what?" Fluffy heaved. She was growing more winded too.

"A dendrochronologist," explained Thermo, "is a scientist who studies tree rings in order to learn what the atmosphere was like in years past. Since our historical temperature records go back no more than 150 years, Dr. Key needs older information to help prove that our warming temperatures are linked to increased carbon dioxide in the atmosphere. Dr. Cape's analysis of the tree rings will help him with that."

Both Fluffy and Puffy were too tired to ask a follow-up question at the moment, so Thermo went on. "It's important for climatologists to know how the climate has been changing, not just for a few hundred years, but for thousands. So in addition to dendrochronology, there's also glaciology. That's where scientists study ice core samples from glaciers. Both glaciology and dendrochronology are part of the broader field of paleoclimatology."

Puffy and Fluffy were becoming sorry they asked. But Puffy still had questions. "How old are these pine tree cores, Thermo? They look like they haven't been part of a living tree for a long time."

"Not since about eight thousand years ago, Puffy," Thermo said matter-of-factly.

"Eight thousand years!" cried Fluffy, unbelieving. "I didn't know we could find any trees, living or not, that had been around that long."

"These samples are from bristlecone pine trees," Thermo told his cloud friends. "Bristlecone pines grow slowly and live a long time. Even the specimens that have been dead awhile can give us information dating back thousands of years."

"What kind of information?" asked Puffy.

"Each ring in the tree core marks one year of the tree's life. Scientists can look at a tree ring and get an idea of temperature and moisture conditions in that year. They can also pick up clues about how climate has changed from the time that tree was alive to today."

As Thermo finished, Fluffy suddenly perked up. "Oh, look down there! It's a circus!"

Sure enough, only a few hundred feet below them, children and their parents were gathered around a big top tent watching an elephant balancing on three legs while holding a ball with its trunk. Nearby, a monkey was performing tricks for its trainer. All the while, a clown in a funny suit was making the children double over with laughter.

"Oh, what fun! Let's go see!" Fluffy called to Thermo and her brother. Suddenly she didn't seem tired at all.

Puffy frowned. "That's going to have to wait, Sis," he said. "I'm exhausted and so are you, though you may not want to admit it. Maybe we can come back after we drop off these tree core samples."

"Aw!" Fluffy pouted, though she conceded that Puffy was probably right about being too tired. Besides, the dry air was continuing to erode her droplets. She kept on forging ahead with her friends.

Just before sunset, the trio arrived at the home of Dr. Julius Cape. Like many other climate scientists, Dr. Cape had moved his research deep into a cave, guarded by a thicket of carbon-dioxide-inhaling kudzu vines.

"These samples are perfect!" exclaimed Dr. Cape, examining the pine tree cores. "The tree rings are in tip-top shape and will be easy for me to read."

"What do you think you'll find, Doctor?" asked Thermo.

"We already suspect that the southwestern United States was a lot drier a thousand years ago," Dr. Cape explained. "These samples can confirm those findings."

"Drier than now?" blurted Puffy. "How do you know?"

"From other historical evidence," replied Dr. Cape. "Apparently the Southwest was the home to several civilizations of Native Americans before the arrival of the Spanish; unfortunately many of those civilizations did not survive." Dr. Cape was concerned about history repeating itself. "I fear that future warming could lead to horrible droughts from California through most of the Rocky Mountains and into the western High Plains. The deserts we have now could grow much larger."

"Heatia would be pleased with that," reasoned Thermo. "No wonder the heat monster is in cahoots with Carbo. He's playing right into Heatia's hands."

"I'm afraid you're right, Thermo," agreed Dr. Cape. "We are going to need to work a lot harder in educating our people if we're going to put a stop to either of them."

That night Thermo, Puffy and Fluffy got some much-needed rest from their laborious journey. The next morning, after a breakfast of jet fuel for Thermo and some ice crystals for Puffy and Fluffy, the three prepared to head west to meet up again with Dr. Key in Hawaii.

"Goodbye, Thermo," waved Dr. Cape. "Goodbye, Puffy and Fluffy, and thank you very much for your help."

"You're welcome, Dr. Cape," answered Fluffy. Then turning to Thermo she asked timidly. "Do you think we could make a short detour back to the circus? I really would like to see that clown."

"Sure," agreed Thermo, winking at Puffy. "I'm always up for a good laugh."

The three friends headed out, looking forward to some rest and relaxation before their next assignment from Dr. Key. Thermo figured they would need it, knowing the tranquility they felt now could quickly change to distress and turmoil later. As he jetted off he thought, *what if he and his allies could not defeat Carbo*?

In the real world, dendrochronology (Greek *dendron* "tree limb," *chronos* "time," and *ology*, "the study of") is the method of dating atmospheric conditions by analyzing tree rings. It dates the time when tree rings formed to the exact calendar year. By examining the tree rings, paleoclimatologists can know temperature and growth patterns in the ancient past, comparing today's temperature and atmospheric conditions over the Earth with that of the past several thousand years.

Story 22: Kilimanjaro

By the middle of 1996 it was obvious to both Thermo and Dr. Key that the cooling trend spawned by the eruption of Mount Pinatubo was gone, and a warming trend had begun once again.

"Even some glaciers are receding," Thermo reported back to Dr. Key, who was in the lab at Mauna Loa, examining the photographs Thermo had taken with his eye-cameras. As the little flying thermometer glided high over the famous Mount Kilimanjaro in Tanzania, Africa, Thermo's eyes snapped photos of the ice that had covered the upper portion of the volcano for thousands of years.

"The views are breathtaking sir," Thermo radioed to Dr. Key, "and as we have heard, much of this glacier appears to be melting too."

Africa was a wondrous sight to behold from above. This time Thermo was without his usual flying partners Fluffy and Puffy, so he was free to explore the mountain and the surrounding countryside. Thermo flew over animal preserves filled with giraffes, zebras and elephants, and observed playful monkeys and colorful birds on the lower slopes of the mountain.

"Go ahead and enjoy the view," Dr. Key said to Thermo, "but watch out for Carbo and his minions. We suspect they are still harassing climate scientists around the world, and they would love to prevent scientists from looking at ice core samples from glaciers like the one you're over."

"Ten-four," answered Thermo. "No sign of Carbo."

"What about Aaliyah and Elimu?" asked Dr. Key. The two humans were paleoclimatologists who had been on the mountain for weeks with their specialized equipment, drilling deep into the glacier to remove cores of ice. The couple planned to analyze the ice later, gathering information about what Earth's climate was like thousands of years ago. Thermo was restricted from encountering most human adults, but Dr. Key had made an exception with these two.

"I think I see them!" Thermo shouted, eyeballing two human figures and heading to a lower altitude to check them out.

Sure enough, it was Aaliyah and Elimu, just removing a long cylinder of ice drawn from a hole that took them weeks to drill. As Thermo hovered above the woman and the man, the two scientists stared up at the sky, not believing their eyes. They had never seen a flying thermometer before.

"Do I see what I think I see?" asked Elimu, bewildered.

"That depends on what you think you see," answered an equally stupefied Aaliyah. "But if it's what I think I see, then yes, I see it!"

"It's okay!" called Thermo from the air. "Dr. Key sent me to look after you as you do your work. I am keeping an eye out for Carbo."

Once Aaliyah and Elimu were satisfied they weren't dreaming, they introduced themselves and showed the flying instrument how they removed and stored the ancient ice cores.

"See those air bubbles inside the core?" Aaliyah said. "We'll analyze that trapped air and see how much carbon dioxide it contains. Then we'll be able to compare it to the CO_2 concentrations in the air today. We'll measure other gases in the ice to help us determine what temperatures were like thousands of years ago."

Aaliyah and Elimu also showed Thermo some before-and-after photographs they had taken, illustrating how quickly the glaciers on Kilimanjaro were shrinking.

"It has happened so fast!" observed Thermo as he continued to scan the atmosphere for the villainous Carbo or one of his henchmen. There was no sign of them, and Thermo wondered aloud, "Maybe Carbo is getting tired of pestering scientists. Maybe he's getting tired of worrying about me."

Still, Thermo had an uneasy feeling as he and the two human scientists made their way down the slopes of Kilimanjaro with their ice cores. Was Carbo up to something that neither he nor Dr. Key could envision? The little thermometer continued to ponder the question all the way down the mountain.

On his long journey home from Africa, Thermo had a lot of time to think. After seeing firsthand what scientists had discovered in tree rings, temperatures and glaciers, Thermo said to himself, "With evidence this convincing, surely humans will see the problem and insist on leaving fossil fuels in the ground. Our battle may be over soon!" Thermo couldn't wait to share his reasoning with Dr. Key.

Back in Hawaii after a delicious home-cooked jet fuel meal,

Thermo told his creator what was on his mind. "Dr. Key, I think we have won. It's obvious to me that once humans look at the scientific data, they will change their habits and stop releasing Carbo's minions into the atmosphere."

Dr. Key sighed. "Ah Thermo. It's time for another lesson in human nature. It may seem odd, but when it comes to bad news, we humans have a tendency to deny reality and hide from it."

Thermo looked puzzled. "I know the news about a warming world is not good," he admitted, "but are you saying that humans won't accept it?"

"Not right away," Dr. Key replied. "Before most humans will be willing to change their lifestyles enough to defeat Carbo, I believe they will go through what psychologists call 'the five stages of grief.'"

"Grief?" inquired Thermo. "What are they grieving for?"

"For the way things were before," explained Dr. Key, "and for the way they want them to be. Most people are not comfortable with change, so first there will be denial. They will think, or at least hope, that scientists are wrong about why the Earth is warming. Once they realize there is a serious problem, the second stage will be the old blame game. When climate change personally affects them, people will lash out in anger at those who have caused their suffering."

"It may take a while before the effects are obvious," observed Thermo, "and by then it may be too late."

"Correct, Son," said Dr. Key. "It may not even happen until well into the 21st century. Then we will see the third stage of grief, what psychologists usually call 'bargaining.' World leaders and fossil fuel companies will try to cling to their old business models, thinking that they can make a few greener and cleaner changes, while continuing to drill for oil and burn coal. They'll eventually get to the next stage, which is depression."

"Oh no!" cried Thermo. "You mean humans will just give up?"

"Some probably will," agreed Dr. Key. "Many citizens and government officials may throw up their hands sometime in the 21st century and say, 'things have gotten so bad, what's the point of doing anything?' But you can't let those people get you down, Thermo. Most will ultimately get to the fifth stage, which is acceptance. Then and only then will Carbo be defeated. When humanity fully accepts the science and the causes of global warming, the carbon pollution problem will stop. And the faster humanity goes through these five stages of grief, the better off they will be."

Thermo stared at Dr. Key, trying to take all this in. He knew that human brains did not work like computers, but he had no idea how illogical the thought processes coming out of them could be.

Eventually Thermo spoke. "It looks like I've been mistaken, Dr. Key. This war with Carbo is going to be very long indeed."

Paleoclimatologists' examinations of ice cores taken from the North Ice Field Glacier of Mount Kilimanjaro indicate that a continuous ice cap has been covering the north face of Kilimanjaro for over 11,000 years. Since 1912 more than 80% of the ancient ice cover on Kilimanjaro has vanished, and scientists predict that Kilimanjaro will become ice-free by the middle of the 21st century. There is much debate over the cause of the Mount Kilimanjaro's ice loss, but most climatologists agree that climate change is probably the biggest contributor.

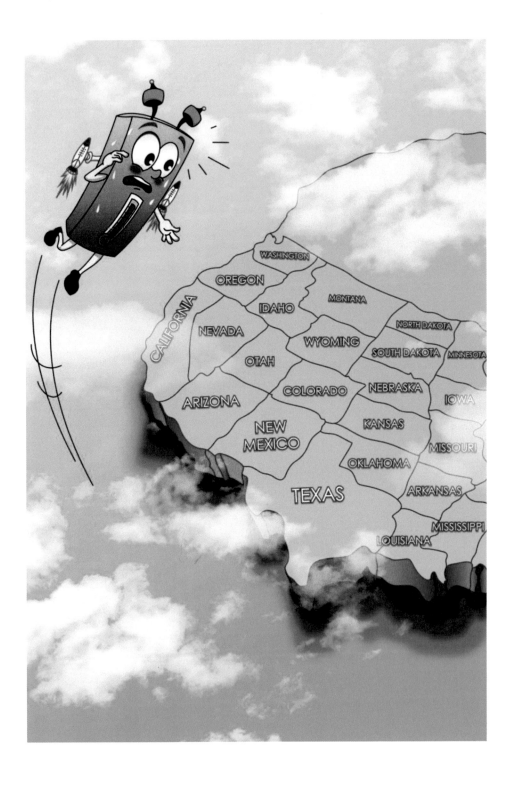

Story 23: The Baby Ramps Up the Heat

Deep inside his Hawaiian cave laboratory on Mauna Loa, Dr. Key sat in his usual comfy office chair staring at a computer monitor. The doctor, however, was anything but comfortable. He called out to his creation, "Thermo, get your lazy apparatus over here and take a look at this."

Thermo knew by now that when his maker was cranky, he should do what he's told. The living thermometer snapped to attention but tried to lighten the mood. "What's up, Doc?" he joked.

Dr. Key was not amused. "Here it is 1997 and I'm getting some oceanographic information the likes of which I haven't seen since 1983. Look at these water temperature readings from north of Australia to the coast of South America," he said, pointing to the computer screen.

Thermo stared at the images, not comprehending. "What do they mean, sir?" he asked.

"I think it's time for a little science lesson, Son," proclaimed the doctor. "Ever hear of El Niño?"

In fact Thermo had heard the words before. He ventured a guess. "I think it means 'the baby boy' in Spanish."

"That's a good start," admired Dr. Key. "Now, do you know what oceanographers are?"

Thermo definitely knew the answer to this one. "They study the ocean; they examine fish and other underwater life, but they're also interested in tides, ocean waves, the ocean's salt content and ocean temperatures too."

"That's right," said Key, obviously pleased. Then he returned to lecture mode. "When sea surface temperatures are above average off the northwest coast of South America out through the Pacific Ocean, the phenomenon is called El Niño. It's something that happens every few years."

Thermo tried to grasp the definition. "So what is it called when the ocean temperatures are cooler in that area?" he quizzed.

"Ah, glad you asked, boy," replied the doctor. "That is called La Niña. Both are part of the El Niño–Southern Oscillation."

"Wow, that's a mouthful," laughed Thermo. "Can I just call it ENSO?"

Dr. Key grinned. "Actually, most scientists do. And these phases of the ENSO will help determine weather patterns throughout the world. From what I see right now, a strong El Niño is on its way."

"Do you think that will help warm the Earth the way Carbo and his carbon friends are doing?" Thermo wanted to know.

"Ah, Thermo my boy, watch and learn." Dr. Key got up and stood next to a large television monitor. "I am going to place a call on my secure line to a young oceanographer friend of mine in Australia. We'll have our usual argument about strong El Niños and the global warming trend."

"Why an argument?" asked Thermo, not understanding.

Dr. Key smiled. "Even though most scientists agree that climate change is occurring, not all agree on the details. That's the case with my Aussie friend and me." With that, he made the call.

Almost immediately, a young bronzed figure appeared on the screen. He looked to be standing in a cave himself. Thermo guessed, correctly, that oceanographers had to hide from the wrath of Carbo too, if their studies were also verifying global warming.

"Dundee!" greeted Dr. Key. "It's nice to see the boy professor again!"

"G'day mate!" Dundee responded. "How's it goin'?"

"I see you've got a great tan again," teased Dr. Key. "You need to spend a little less time surfing and more time cataloguing temperature readings from your ocean buoys."

"Blimey, Key, you old taskmaster!" Dundee shot back. "You know I've been working on an ENSO forecast night and day for six months now. I have to let off some steam somehow!"

"Calm down, boy," soothed Dr. Key. "Tell me what you've got."

"No worries, Key. But it looks like a sweet El Niño is in the making. The thing should spike temperatures over most of the world in 1998 if it's big enough."

Dr. Key snickered. "Well my boy," he began, stirring the pot, "a record El Niño would propel average temperatures to new all-time levels for sure. Then those temperatures will stick around until the next strong El Niño lifts them even higher."

"No no no, Key!" Dundee cried. "How many times must we go over this? Strong El Niño years will only mean temporary warming.

They are not stepping-stones to a higher plane of warmth! You claim that El Niños will become stronger or more frequent due to climate change, but that is simply not the case!"

"I tell you what," proposed Dr. Key, "I'll send out my special instrument Thermo to measure this El Niño event over the next year or so. We'll just see if El Niños don't get stronger in the long run. I'll let you know what I find."

"I'm sure you will, Key," Dundee came back. "I'm sure you will."

"Goodbye, Dundee," smiled Dr. Key. "It's been good sparring with you again."

"Cheers, mate!" called out Dundee, and then the screen went dark.

"And that, my boy," chuckled Dr. Key, "is how you keep those young whippersnapper professors on their toes. I guess it's up to you now to find out who's right, Dundee or yours truly."

So Thermo began taking air temperature readings near the El Niño zone in the Pacific, measuring how the extra heat from the ocean transferred into the atmosphere. Later, hovering over the United States for several days, Thermo's chest thermometer continually turned bright red. He noticed a big jump in temperatures at almost every location. In fact, El Niño produced record-setting warmth throughout the world.

There were both winners and losers from El Niño. Heatia the heat monster basked in the glory of the increased warmth. For Phoon, 1997 was a mixed blessing. Warmer ocean waters helped produce strong tropical cyclones in the Pacific, but vigorous tropical storms in the Atlantic were few. That's because El Niño also created forceful wind shear in the high altitudes above the Atlantic. That tended to keep tropical cyclones weak there, if they formed at all.

Carbo the Carbon Dioxide Molecule didn't like El Niño one bit. He worried that the extra heat it brought might finally wake humans up to the reality of a warming Earth.

That subject was on Thermo's mind once he was back at the Mauna Loa laboratory. "Don't you think the warmer temperatures will make humans want to finally do something?" Thermo asked Dr. Key.

"I don't know," replied the doctor. "Things have to get pretty bad before humans force themselves to change. Since it's not hot enough to kill many people, I have a hunch that no one will really take notice."

As it turned out, Dr. Key's hunch was, unfortunately, exactly right.

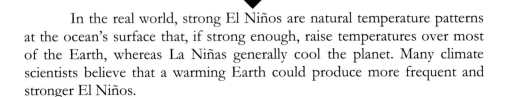

In the real world, strong El Niños are natural temperature patterns at the ocean's surface that, if strong enough, raise temperatures over most of the Earth, whereas La Niñas generally cool the planet. Many climate scientists believe that a warming Earth could produce more frequent and stronger El Niños.

STORY 24: SKATING ON THIN ICE

I can't believe how warm it is here," Thermo remarked. "I expected a much cooler reception!"

Snowy laughed. "You always did crack me up, Thermo! It's good to see you again."

It was now January 1998 and Thermo had decided to let bygones be bygones and visit Snowy at his Canadian home. He had thought long and hard about what Dr. Key told him—that natural "monsters" have been producing storms, heat waves and blizzards over the Earth since the beginning of time, not necessarily out of spite or anger, but simply because it is their nature to do so. Viewing Snowy's actions from that point of view, Thermo realized that although he didn't like everything the snowman did, he couldn't really blame him for it. Snowy was simply being himself. Instead of trying to fight Snowy or interfere when he was on a rampage, Thermo decided he should just try to stay out of his way and concentrate his energy on fighting the unnatural monsters such as Carbo and his minions.

"I'm looking forward to playing with your snow pals the Flakes," Thermo said eagerly.

"Well, you certainly could if it were colder," replied Snowy, "but that thermometer on your chest tells me that it will be nearly impossible. Normally this time of year I can easily set the Flakes loose from Toronto in eastern Canada down to New England in the United States. But not right now. They wouldn't survive in this warmth."

"Maybe if we scouted around somewhere else, we might find a place that's cold enough for them to play," suggested Thermo.

"That's a good idea," agreed Snowy. "Let's take my sleigh over to Montreal in Quebec. Can you speak French in case we encounter some humans?"

"Où est le froid?" Thermo said with a perfect accent. "Where is the cold?"

Snowy laughed again. "Wonderful, Thermo! Let's go!"

As the two sailed over the unfrozen Canadian countryside, there was no doubt in Thermo's mind that Carbo had a hand in producing the warm weather. The temperature readings he picked up showed near-freezing numbers from Ontario eastward to Nova Scotia. Near-freezing yes, but this was an area that would usually see much colder wintertime temperatures. Twenties down to below zero Fahrenheit would be more typical this time of year.

"What's the temperature on the ground?" Snowy asked.

Thermo checked his readings again. "It is right at freezing," he replied.

"And way up here where we are?" Snowy asked.

"We're well below freezing at this level," Thermo answered.

Snowy thought about that. "Then there's no reason why I can't make some snow!" And the snowman began to release a multitude of Flakes from the clouds.

As the Flakes happily emerged, they saw Thermo and beamed, "Hi, Thermo! Want to play?"

"You bet!" answered the jubilant thermometer, and Thermo began to jet up and down through the delighted Flakes, engaging in an impromptu game of tag. As the Flakes continued to fall toward the ground, their glee suddenly turned to fear.

"We're getting wet!" the Flakes wailed.

Snowy and Thermo's laughter turned to alarm.

"We're melting!" the Flakes cried in unison, their high-pitched squeals filling the air.

"Thermo!" scolded Snowy, "I thought you said it was freezing all the way from here to the ground!"

"No," objected Thermo, "I said it was freezing up here and freezing at the ground. There must be a layer of warmer air in between!" It was too late for Snowy to stop releasing the Flakes, and the little six-sided crystals kept falling, melting, and turning to liquid, then once on the ground, re-freezing to everything they touched.

Suddenly without warning, a familiar face appeared in the sky, startling Thermo and Snowy into momentary silence. Then Thermo spoke. "Skates!" The flying thermometer had not seen the ice monster since 1973, but Thermo knew that whenever Skates was near, trouble was soon to follow.

"Hello, Snowy. Hi, little thermometer. Bet you're surprised to see me this far north in January, huh?" Skates sneered.

It went without saying that they were.

"As you see," Skates boasted, "I have created a warm layer in our weather cake: freezing temperatures above and freezing temperatures below, but right in the middle, a nice slice of air just warm enough to melt your little Flakes so they can change over to ice on the freezing ground below. Look down and behold my catastrophic creation!"

Both Snowy and Thermo knew what they would see even before they looked. Tree limbs weighed down under coatings of thick ice, power lines sagged, streets and highways were littered with crashed cars sliding over the slick roads. The pair watched as lights blinked off from Ontario to Maine, the power outages stretching as far as they could see.

A warm air layer this far north in January could mean only one thing: Skates was getting some help from Carbo the Carbon Dioxide Molecule. Only he and his minions would be able to warm the Earth enough to allow Skates an opportunity to use that warm air to create an ice storm. Snowy was re-thinking his decision to befriend Skates. Thermo was re-thinking his decision not to interfere with destructive weather. Discouraged, they both decided in the end to leave the icy scene behind.

After traveling for several hundred miles, Thermo spoke first. "Snowy, I need to head back to Hawaii to report this to Dr. Key in person."

"I understand," Snowy said reluctantly. "It was good to see you, even if my Flakes did help create an ice storm."

"It was great seeing you too, Snowy," said Thermo. "Goodbye for now. Try not to cause any more trouble, okay?"

Snowy nodded, not promising anything. "Goodbye Thermo," he said, and his sleigh pulled by eight tiny clouds rose into the sky and was gone.

Thermo would have more bad news for Dr. Key.

In the real world, the North American Ice Storm of January 1998 struck in Canada from eastern Ontario to southern Quebec to Nova Scotia, and in the United States from northern New York to central Maine. It is possible that a warming world helped cause this storm to form so far north.

Story 25: Face Off Over a Hockey Stick

Oh, my aching back!" Dr. Key grimaced as he sat up on the edge of his bed. The good doctor was getting on in years, and the early-morning backaches were becoming more common. "Joshua, could you bring me a cup of tea please?"

The year was 1999. Thermo the flying thermometer was about his usual task of taking temperature readings around the world and had recently flown over Antarctica. Dr. Key wondered how Thermo was faring, and once on his feet, the doctor slowly shuffled over to his computer.

"Splendid," he whispered, his mood improving as he reviewed Thermo's latest reports. "He's been making good headway." Dr. Key then began his morning ritual of digging through encrypted web sites to retrieve the latest findings from fellow climate scientists, confirming that the recent warming trends around the globe were continuing. Suddenly he spotted something that made him jump, sending a sharp pain up his back again.

"Ow!" Dr. Key moaned.

"Your back, sir?" Joshua asked, handing the doctor his morning tea.

"Yes, Joshua. I mean, no." Dr. Key paused, collecting himself. "I mean, here's what made me jump," and he pointed toward the computer screen. It was a new paper published by the scientific journal *Geophysical Research Letters*. "Look at the graph that accompanies this article," Dr. Key showed Joshua.

Joshua, not really sure of what he was looking at, commented, "It looks like a hockey stick."

"Yes it does," affirmed Dr. Key. "Look closely at the pattern on the graph; the handle portion of the hockey stick shows a relatively flat and sometimes downward temperature trend, beginning a thousand years ago to around 1900. The stick's blade shape represents a sharp upward spike of warming temperatures projected for the future." Dr. Key looked at the name of the document's author. "Who is this brash young Dr. Geoffrey White? Surely he can't be right. If his study is correct, then more than likely, civilization is doomed."

"Doomed?" Joshua gulped.

Dr. Key continued reading the study. "This article has been reviewed by many other scientists who support the research, so there is obviously something to it. I need to meet this Dr. Geoffrey White."

Dr. White received Key's invitation to visit Hawaii through covert coded communication, preventing Carbo and his minions from discovering the location of the Mauna Loa laboratory. When Dr. White arrived at the airport, Joshua discretely drove the young scientist to the secret cave.

"Very impressive," Dr. White commented as he entered the vast underground domain. He looked around, admiring the cave's antique furnishings and the fine art on its walls.

"If you'll excuse me, sir," said Joshua, "I'll go fetch Dr. Key from his afternoon nap."

As Dr. White waited, he wondered exactly what this meeting was all about. He knew that Dr. Key did not agree with some of his findings. But he also knew the doctor was a climatologist like himself and was interested in discovering the full truth about Carbo and his molecule minions. So he was not prepared when Dr. Key stormed into the room in the foulest of moods. White stood and extended his hand, but Dr. Key brushed it away.

"What the devil is this, boy?" Dr. Key barked. "I am appalled. The main chart associated with your findings looks like a hockey stick. I know we don't play much hockey in Hawaii, but I know a hockey stick when I see one. Even my butler recognized it. You know what this means, don't you? If you are right, it means the end of humanity."

Taken aback, the young Dr. White said with a hint of sarcasm, "Glad to meet you too, Dr. Key. I'm impressed with your consistent and timely carbon dioxide readings from this mountain. I know that the global temperature trend on my graph is startling, but every other climatologist who reviewed the study comes to the same conclusion. Temperature measurements around the globe are beginning to confirm the trend. What Carbo and his minions are doing could very well mean the end of humankind."

Dr. Key inhaled, preparing for another loud and lengthy retort, but just then Thermo appeared, back from his travels. The doctor hadn't planned on letting his guest know about Thermo and was shocked to see him.

Dr. White reacted as if he were looking at a ghost. "Is that a l-living thermometer?" he sputtered.

Thermo turned off his jets and stood there, silent.

Through clenched teeth, Dr. Key said, "This is my special secret instrument that keeps tabs on the planet's temperature. He'll confirm whether or not your outrageous findings are accurate. But if you breathe a word of his existence to anyone, I'll come after you with a lot more than a hockey stick!"

Dr. White's face reddened. "Your machine runs on jet fuel?" he challenged. "Don't you know that jet engines release carbon? Even your research instrument is polluting the atmosphere!"

For several moments the two men glared at one another in an extended stare-down, and then Dr. Key broke the tension with a heavy sigh. "You are right, boy. That has bothered me for some time. Perhaps you can help me find an alternative fuel." Then he grinned. "You and I are on the same team you know. Let's take a break from this heavy topic. Joshua, would you bring us some tea?"

The two scientists sat down and talked about more pleasant matters: where they grew up, where they went to school, fascinating people they had met. As the pair continued to chat, they discovered they had much in common. As the hours ticked by, they continued to share their stories and jokes. Gradually the conversation turned back to the subject at hand, but this time with a much more harmonious tone. Both men agreed that Carbo was to blame for the hockey stick graph's dire predictions and that he must be defeated. They also recognized that to do so would take not only a long-term campaign of public education, but also a turn toward green energy and a move away from relying on fossil fuels such as oil and gas and coal.

Later as the scientists said their goodbyes, Thermo returned to extend his final greetings.

"Dr. White," Thermo asked hesitantly, "I would ask you again, please do not tell anyone about me."

"I won't," promised Dr. White. Then turning to Dr. Key, he asked, "But will you share your thermometer's findings with me? I think they would benefit the entire climate community."

Dr. Key agreed. "Yes, I suppose that's a good idea."

Now, Thermo thought, *my work will have an even wider audience.* He was doing his job, and more than ever, he knew that job had great value.

In the real world, the character of Dr. Geoffrey White is inspired by Dr. Michael Mann, who, in 1998, wrote a peer-reviewed paper through *Geophysical Research Letters* that included what became known as the "Hockey Stick Graph," showing global temperatures warming at a very high rate. A peer-reviewed paper is one that is read and approved by many individuals to gain scientific acceptance. Most publications that deny climate change do not have peer-reviewed credentials.

STORY 26: Y2K CHAD-CHASM

Dawn broke the morning of January 1, 2000 after a very long night. Dr. Key was still in his clothes, having never gone to bed.

"Is the tea ready?" he asked his butler.

"Coming up," Joshua answered, yawning. He had not slept at all either.

"Thank you for all your help checking the software last night, Joshua," Dr. Key called. "I know I spoiled your big start-of-the-new-millennium festivities." Then he added, "Though technically I believe the millennium won't occur until next year."

"Thank you," Joshua replied. "Going through all that computer code to see if there were any Y2K problems took me another twelve hours, but as you can see, there are no issues and the lights are on." Then he added with a smile, "You can pay me back next year in extra champagne."

Just then Thermo dragged in, also showing signs of fatigue.

"Thermo!" a relieved Dr. Key exclaimed. "How is everything in Europe and North America? Any computer problems?"

"No, sir. Everything looks good," reported Thermo. "Not even minor power outages."

Humans all over the world had been concerned that their computers would not discern what to do when the date transitioned from 1999 to 2000 because of old calendar software, and technology experts had spent billions of dollars preventing a software nightmare for civilization. A quick trip around the globe told Thermo there were no turn-of-the-century glitches from the Y2K changeover.

"Glad to hear it," smiled Dr. Key. "Thank you."

Thermo, Dr. Key and Joshua made some more small talk, but soon realized they had better go to bed sometime. Dozing much of the day, they slept securely in the hopes that civilization had survived the dawn of the new century, and for now might even be safe from Carbo and his molecular minions. Waking up in time for some traditional football bowl games, the three spent the evening celebrating their good fortune.

Several thousand miles away, Carbo was not celebrating. "The last few years have not been good for us," he admitted to his main minions, Toasty and Roasty. "Humans are starting to listen to climate scientists. Then there's that awful Kyoto Protocol. The treaty committed way too many countries to reducing the release of our friends."

"At least we kept the United States out of it," Toasty offered. "For now."

"Yes, that's something," agreed Carbo. "But that U.S. President Clinton is on to us, and his vice president is running to succeed him in office. We need to do something."

Just then, another of Carbo's minions dashed in breathlessly. "Carbo, Carbo!" he yelled. "I believe we may be in luck!"

Carbo looked doubtful. His minions rarely had any good ideas. Still he asked hopefully, "What do you have, Flame?"

"A Texas oil man is running for President against Al Bore."

"That's Al Gore," Carbo corrected.

"Right, Gore," repeated Flame. "Anyway, if we can help get the Texan George Bush elected, we'd have a much better chance of keeping the country relying on fossil fuels."

"And a much better chance of getting more of our friends released," added Toasty.

"Yes," said Carbo, "and since U.S. influence is still world-wide, that would go a long way in keeping the transition to clean energy at bay."

"But what if Gore wins?" Roasty asked innocently. "That would be bad, right?"

Carbo liked Roasty, but most of the time he was denser than a bar of platinum. "Yes, that would be bad, Roasty," replied Carbo patiently. "That man has become a big thorn in my side." Carbo hated to admit failure in front of his minions, but as of yet he had not been able to fool the Vice President into discounting the destructive power of a trillion released carbon dioxide molecules.

"Yeah," confirmed Roasty, "and ever since Gore invented that Internet thing, the word about us is spreading."

Carbo looked down at Roasty pitifully. "Roasty, Al Gore did not invent....oh never mind. But yes, climate scientists have a much bigger voice now that they can communicate with so many other humans online."

"So what do we do, boss?" ventured Toasty.

"We have to get the oil man elected, guys," Carbo said. "Put Bush's name in the minds of the voters. But keep the election close. If we can create a polarized public, we can confuse the humans. There will be a wide chasm between the green energy crowd and those too lazy to change."

Carbo's loyal henchmen became the best campaign managers a candidate ever had. They split the country into regions, and each minion took charge of get-out-the-vote efforts in his respective area of the country. The molecules whispered Bush's praises in the ears of voters far and wide, helping to convince thousands of them that the Texan was the best man for the job. Carbo himself took charge of the candidates' second televised debate, causing Gore to bumble through it and lose even more support.

When Election Day came, the carbon dioxide molecules waited with bated breath, realizing the outcome might determine their very existence.

"I'm nervous," admitted Flame.

"It's so close!" worried Toasty.

"I can't look, boss!" cried Roasty.

"Don't worry, guys," soothed a composed Carbo. "We've done our job in every part of the country, influencing voters from Arizona to New Hampshire, from Idaho to Florida."

"Florida?" Toasty and Roasty and Flame asked at the same time.

"You took care of Florida, right?" Carbo challenged.

The three minions looked at one another, then down at the floor, not able to meet Carbo's eye. Carbo just sighed and shook his head. The Florida vote was too close to call.

The votes had been cast, so the molecule minions could do little more than watch and wait as the poll results in Florida were counted again and all paper ballots were examined to see if the punched-out portions or "chads" indicated a vote for one candidate or the other.

Weeks went by with no outcome, and when the election produced legal challenges, Carbo spent his time buzzing around the Supreme Court, picking the justices' brains and stealthily urging them to make up their minds in his favor.

At last the day arrived. "Time to celebrate, guys!" Carbo declared to his minions when Bush was finally announced the winner by a slim margin.

"Our friends are safe!" applauded Flame.

"We won!" Toasty exulted.

"I thought Bush won," said Roasty, confused as usual.

The party was on. As the carbon carousing went on all night, Carbo was at the center of it all, laughing, joking and sipping his oxygen-spiked punch. But even as he smiled and partied through the gala festivities, Carbo had to wonder if the joyous celebration might only be temporary.

In the real world, there were no unseen forces swaying the election of 2000, but when the last vote was counted, only 537 votes separated Climate Change activist Al Gore from victor George Bush.

STORY 27: HYBRIDS AND HOSTILITIES

"These new cars are starting to give me fits," said Carbo the Carbon Dioxide Molecule to his molecule minions as they flitted around a huge auto dealership.

"What's the problem, boss?" asked Roasty. "The cars still use gasoline, don't they?"

"Yes," replied Carbo, "but you haven't been paying attention, have you?" he demanded.

"Who is Attention? And how much should I pay him?" the clueless carbon minion genuinely wanted to know.

Carbo sighed, deciding to let it pass and simply continue. "The humans have come up with a way of allowing some newer cars to run on battery power much of the time so they use a lot less gasoline. The cars are called hybrids. As long as they're around, fewer of our friends will get released into the atmosphere."

"Aren't those cars pretty expensive?" asked Toasty. "Surely their cost will keep most people from buying them."

"Not anymore," Carbo said sadly. "Unfortunately they've been making cheaper hybrid cars since at least 1997. It's now 2002 and those awful machines are becoming much more common. That Prius alone is wrecking my plans to get all of our friends released." Then the chief carbon dioxide molecule ventured hesitantly, "Any ideas, guys?"

Roasty and Toasty tried to think, and although it hurt a little, an idea started forming in Roasty's molecule-sized brain. "Maybe we could have the humans go to war and have all the hybrid cars bombed," he suggested.

Toasty chuckled scornfully, but Carbo perked up. "Actually, a war is a good idea," he considered.

"It is?" asked a dumbfounded Roasty.

"Yes," answered Carbo, "except we need to have the United States start a war with a country that has lots of oil."

Roasty wasn't following. "How would that get rid of the hybrids, boss?"

"It wouldn't get rid of them completely, but if the U.S. can get oil more cheaply, there will be no need for people to buy them," Carbo lectured.

Toasty tried out a theory. "Iraq has lots of oil, right?"

"Yes," Carbo said, seeing where this was headed.

"I guess so," said Roasty, not really sure.

"And President Bush thinks that country might have a lot of dangerous weapons, right?" Toasty added.

"Right!" confirmed Carbo.

"Who?" blinked Roasty.

"But how do we get the U.S. and Iraq into battle?" asked Toasty.

"That should be easy," Carbo declared. "The American humans are bloodthirsty after that 911 thing. They're willing to strike almost any Arab nation in the Middle East. Roasty, thank you for such a great idea!"

Roasty had no idea what a war with Iraq had to do with his idea, but he simply decided that instead of asking, he would just accept the compliment and smile.

So Carbo and his minions spread the word to other carbon dioxide molecules who, in turn, whizzed around the brains of all the politicians they could find, and by 2003 the war with Iraq was on.

Unfortunately for Carbo, the war did not lead to cheaper oil as he had hoped, and sales of hybrid vehicles continued to climb.

"Curses! This will never do," Carbo complained to Toasty and Roasty.

"No, boss, it won't, it just won't do at all," Roasty repeated. "Do you want me to think of another idea?"

"Knock yourself out," Carbo told him.

Roasty didn't understand that plan, but he complied anyway, remaining unconscious for the rest of the day.

In the real world, hybrid automobiles became more common after the turn of the 21st century. The fuel efficiency of conventional autos also improved.

Some observers think that one of the main reasons the United States and Britain went to war against Saddam Hussein's dictatorial regime in Iraq was the hope of obtaining cheap energy. However, the West never saw the price of gasoline fall significantly after the war ended.

Story 28: Fuel Gets Corny

"Can you drop down to a lower altitude, Thermo?" Dr. Key asked the flying thermometer over his two-way radio from the lab in Mauna Loa. "I would like to see the corn close up."

Dr. Key was monitoring Thermo's excursion over a huge Iowa cornfield through the remote cameras that served as his creation's eyes. His cumulus cloud pals Puffy and Fluffy were along for the ride.

"Let's see if the two of you can get closer to the ground without evaporating," Thermo suggested to his friends.

"Lowering our altitude," Puffy called.

"Right behind you," Fluffy echoed.

"How's this level, sir?" Thermo asked Dr. Key.

"That's good," said Dr. Key as Thermo soared over the field of ripe yellow corn, its stalks gently swaying in the summer breeze. Puffy and Fluffy took in the pastoral scene, while nearby a combine harvester picked the ripe ears of corn and almost magically separated the golden kernels from the corncobs that held them.

"This is the corniest place I have ever seen," observed Fluffy.

"I'll bet I have something even cornier," said Thermo with a smile sneaking across his metal face.

"What's that?" asked Fluffy.

"Well," asked Thermo, "why was six afraid of seven?"

"What?" asked Fluffy, puzzled. "I don't know!"

"Because seven ate nine!" Thermo laughed.

Fluffy groaned.

Puffy smiled, "Well, you're right Thermo, that is corny!"

Dr. Key came back on the two-way radio. "Thermo, could you fly over those large buildings in the distance? I believe that is where workers turn the corn into alcohol."

Puffy spotted a large sign on one of the buildings that read "Distillery." He pointed. "There, Thermo, that's the place."

Thermo knew that Dr. Key's interest in this corn-to-alcohol process had nothing to do with farming or food or manufacturing beverages. This operation produced ethanol fuel, a mixture of alcohol and gasoline to power cars and trucks, and maybe even Thermo's own jet engines. The mixture was designed to reduce the amount of oil pumped out of the ground. To Dr. Key, this seemed particularly useful, since it also meant less carbon dioxide would be released into the atmosphere.

"Have you seen any sign of Carbo or his minions, Thermo?" Dr. Key asked. The doctor knew that if Carbo had even a hint that Thermo was investigating the ethanol plant, the molecule might try to interfere.

"I haven't seen any evidence of him," Thermo replied as he landed at the distillery. "Maybe he doesn't want to get too close to these corn stalks. All of them take in CO_2 and the last thing Carbo wants is to be trapped inside a plant."

"You're probably right," agreed the doctor, and then he asked, "Any chance of sneaking inside the building? I would love to see the process of turning corn into alcohol."

Thermo had strict orders to steer clear of human adults, so he quickly hid as a group of them walked by. When they were gone, he called to his cumulus cloud friends, "You two stay up there and stand guard. Let me know if you see any sign of Carbo." Then, Thermo carefully opened the door to the distillery and slipped inside.

Before him were huge tanks filled with corn. He watched, as first the grain was soaked in water, then heated with steam. Inside the tanks the food starches were gradually converted to sugars and the resulting concoction left to ferment. Later, the mush was heated again until the alcohol evaporated and was captured in special tubing, ready to be mixed with gasoline.

"Splendid!" Dr. Key exclaimed, watching the process through Thermo's camera eyes. "I must try to patch in my young climatologist friend Dr. Geoffrey White. He would love to see this."

While Thermo waited, Dr. Key pushed a few buttons on his console in Mauna Loa, and in minutes Dr. White was able to see the images from Thermo's cameras at his own laboratory in Pennsylvania.

"Very impressive," White told Dr. Key. "If we can replace some of the need for oil with this renewable energy resource from corn, we might be able to limit Carbo's influence and slow the rate of global warming. Perhaps my hockey stick graph was premature after all. Besides," he added with a smile, "it's a gluten-free alternative!"

Dr. Key let out a hearty laugh. "Just don't drink it!" he joked back.

"Speaking of Carbo," White said, "I would think that evil carbon dioxide molecule or one of his henchmen would try to disrupt the ethanol operation before long. Surely he and his kind are threatened by it."

"That's what I thought too," Dr. Key agreed. "But so far there is no sign of him. It's almost like he knows something we don't know and is staying away."

Dr. Key was only half correct, for just out of Thermo's vision, Carbo and his main minions Toasty and Roasty watched every move the flying thermometer made, and they heard every word Thermo reported back to his maker and instructor.

"Aren't you going to move in and stop all this?" Toasty asked.

"Why should I?" Carbo sneered as he watched the workers busily occupied with the ethanol manufacturing. "They don't scare me. Let them have their little fun, because what they think is a mountain of environmental progress is no more than a molehill to us. We have much bigger battles to fight." Then he let out a sinister chuckle.

Carbo's two half-witted minions didn't really understand their boss, but after looking questioningly at one another for a second they began to chuckle as well, simply because it felt good to do it.

In the real world, environmentalists and climatologists initially hailed ethanol fuel as a valuable alternative to power all vehicles. By 2010, however, many experts began to doubt its value, claiming that it took almost a gallon of fossil fuel to produce a gallon of ethanol. Although almost 14 billion gallons of ethanol fuel are produced from corn every year in the United States, scientists are now looking to other, possibly more energy-efficient sources of ethanol fuel, including sugar cane, sugar beets, switch grass and algae.

STORY 29: TRÈS CHAUD

It had been a long time since Heatia had seen such an opportunity. As the heat monster surveyed the French countryside in the summer of 2003, she relished in what she found. *In all my wildest, dustiest dreams, there has never been this kind of sinking air and high pressure*, she thought. Heatia began to build a dangerous heat wave that would rival anything she had ever created before.

Back in Mauna Loa, Dr. Key saw the signs. "Thermo," he called to his invention, "heat is building over Europe like I have never seen. I know I risk overheating your machinery, but I need you to look at this first-hand."

Thermo was happy to oblige the doctor, but he wasn't prepared for what greeted him when he landed near the Eiffel Tower in Paris. His thermometer read well into the 90s Fahrenheit, and it wasn't long before he could feel his circuits growing warm. "I have to find some shade, and fast," he whispered. Thermo managed to find a cooler spot behind the famous tower, and was also able to blend in with its metal framework to stay out of sight of the human adults. "Can it get any hotter?" Thermo wondered aloud.

The answer was a definite yes. After exploring Paris and taking temperature readings for two weeks, Thermo saw the numbers build increasingly higher, not only at ground level, but well up into the atmosphere. As air pressure increased at higher altitudes, the sinking air continued to compress and warm the surface temperatures toward record values.

"Heatia must be nearby," Thermo said to himself. "But where?"

On the hottest day so far of his visit, Thermo was flying over the city, when he looked down and could not believe his eyes. Below him was none other than the couple he had met at Mount Kilimanjaro, Aaliyah and Elimu. Thermo immediately dropped to the ground to say hello.

"Thermo!" cried Aaliyah, looking up. "How good to see you!"

"It's wonderful to see you too," replied Thermo. "What brings you to Paris during this scorcher of a summer?"

"We're on vacation in between ice-core extractions," Elimu told Thermo, "but I'm starting to wish we were back on the mountain. I can't believe the heat. Just this morning it was almost too hot to have breakfast at a sidewalk café."

"Would you two do me a favor?" asked Thermo. "Please report to me what you experience among the humans. Dr. Key and I have a bad feeling about this heat wave. It could turn out to be disastrous." After agreeing to meet again before the couple returned to Africa, Aaliyah, Elimu and Thermo parted ways.

Continuing to observe the French capital from above, Thermo witnessed the increasing discomfort of the humans down below. His thermometer consistently read above 100 degrees every afternoon. *Surely Carbo has a hand in this*, he thought.

Thermo searched far and wide for a sign of the heat monster Heatia. He flew over Germany, northward to the Netherlands, and then south into Spain and Italy, but could not catch sight of the thin brown parachute-shaped waif that was wreaking so much havoc.

That's because Heatia was keeping low to the ground. She spent every afternoon baking all the farm crops in the countryside, feeling increasingly empowered. "Thank you, Carbo, wherever you are!" she shouted into the hot wind blasting her face.

When Thermo met again with Aaliyah and Elimu, the burning sidewalks were almost barren of humans in the August afternoons. Most people had gone in search of air-conditioned stores or theatres, or at least the shade of a park. As Thermo, Aaliyah and Elimu walked in the sweltering 100-degree-plus heat, they spotted a flower shop on the corner. Hoping to spend a few minutes in a cooler environment, they ducked inside.

Upon entering the shop, however, they found only a weak fan buzzing in the corner. Without much ventilation in the room, the atmosphere was even more stifling than outside. "Hello," called Aaliyah. "Is anyone here?"

A weak old woman hobbled out of a back room, her dress soaked in sweat. She appeared to be well into her eighties, but still had a warm, though slightly pained, smile.

"Voulez-vous des fleurs?" she asked in short breaths. "Would you like some flowers?"

Elimu politely bought a few roses for Aaliyah and asked the old woman her name.

"Paulette," she replied. "C'est très chaud."

"Yes," Elimu agreed, "it is very hot. Where are you living?"

The woman answered that since her husband passed away she lived in a small apartment in the back of the shop. She had no air conditioning and told the couple that even at night her home was extremely uncomfortable.

Knowing what heat could do to the elderly, Elimu asked her, "Do you have family you can stay with?"

"No," she replied. And even if she did, she told them, she couldn't bring herself to leave her home, even for a day.

Elimu bought more roses in the hopes that Paulette would use the money for an air-conditioned hotel room, and then the couple reluctantly left the old woman. She waved goodbye to them with the same pained and wrinkled smile.

The next day, Elimu and Aaliyah were scheduled to end their vacation and fly home to Africa, but they stopped by the flower shop one more time on their way to the airport. Finding the door locked, they read the sign that had been posted: Fermé, it read. Closed, and a fresh black wreath hung on the door.

"Oh no," Aaliyah moaned. The two feared that like many elderly Parisians that summer, Paulette must have succumbed to the deadly heat.

Near the airport, Elimu and Aaliyah met with Thermo one more time before boarding their flight. Like the couple, he too was devastated about Paulette, and regretted that he could not find Heatia.

"What would you be able to do if you found her?" Aaliyah asked a tearful Thermo.

"Being so little, probably nothing, I guess," said the distraught thermometer, "but I must do something to prevent Carbo from helping that heat monster again."

Aaliyah and Elimu vowed to continue the fight as well, knowing that it would take millions more humans like them to bring about any significant victory in the battle against a warming world.

In the real world, the 2003 European heat wave was the hottest summer on record in Europe's modern history. France was hit especially hard, where just under 15,000 of its citizens died from heat-related causes.

Story 30: Fearsome Foursome

Humans usually associate a conga line with music and dancing and a party atmosphere. But the conga line of destructive hurricanes that the tropical monster Phoon paraded through the state of Florida during the summer of 2004 was a party nobody wanted.

Even before the first hurricane struck, Dr. Key could see it coming. "Do you see the pattern that's developing?" the doctor asked Thermo as they examined the weather maps in the lab at Mauna Loa. "Florida is ripe and ready to get slammed by tropical weather."

Filling up his creation with the doctor's newly developed and environmentally friendly alternative to jet fuel, Dr. Key dispatched Thermo to Florida to monitor the weather conditions there, and to take atmospheric readings that the doctor could forward to the National Hurricane Center. When Thermo arrived in the Sunshine State, he found that Phoon had already sent a tropical storm named Bonnie into Florida's panhandle.

But the worst was yet to come.

"Stay out of Phoon's way, Thermo," instructed Dr. Key over the two-way radio. "Stay high near the jet stream and out of sight."

"That's where I am now," Thermo told the doctor. "Even from up here I can clearly see that Phoon is getting ready for another strike. A hurricane named Charley is headed through the Straits of Florida. That's the waterway between Cuba and the Florida Keys."

Dr. Key chuckled. He knew where the Straits of Florida were. As he eyeballed a map of Charley's expected path, his smile suddenly disappeared. "Once the hurricane is in the Gulf of Mexico, watch for it to turn back toward the Florida coast. This one's going to do some damage."

Sure enough, Phoon turned Charley toward Florida, carrying with it powerful 145 mph winds. Thermo watched in horror as hundreds of thousands of homes lost power, more than two thousand buildings were leveled, and much of the state's orange crop was ruined.

"You can't stop this from happening, Thermo," reminded Dr. Key. "Don't try to do battle with Phoon."

Thermo knew Dr. Key was right, so he continued to watch helplessly from his high perch until the hurricane was gone.

Even while Florida was still recovering from Charley's onslaught, another hurricane raced into Florida with winds exceeding 100 mph. Its name was Frances, and it brought damage to thousands of homes before emerging into the Gulf of Mexico and turning northward to flood a path from Georgia to Pennsylvania.

"How much can Florida take?" Thermo asked Dr. Key over the two-way.

"I guess we'll find out, Son, because another hurricane is headed its way."

Only a few days later, Hurricane Ivan destroyed thousands of homes in the Florida panhandle with its 120 mph winds.

"This is too much!" wailed Thermo.

But much more was yet to come. Just nine days later, a hurricane named Jeanne was duplicating the path Frances had traveled a week before, and was closing in on the same area already plundered by the prior hurricane. Thermo couldn't help himself, and swooped down to a lower altitude, risking detection by Phoon.

What he saw made him cringe. Just below him on the beach a crowd had gathered around a beautiful woman in a white dress and a handsome gentleman in a tuxedo.

"It's a wedding!" cried Thermo, surprised and more than a little frightened. The two young humans were gazing into one another's eyes, oblivious to everything else around them, including Phoon's tropical terror that was quickly bearing down on the couple and their guests.

"Dr. Key!" Thermo called to his maker on the two-way radio. "Come in, Dr. Key!"

"Key here. What's the problem, Thermo?"

"Hurricane Jeanne is headed into Florida and a couple is getting married on the beach! I've got to warn them!"

"Thermo, you know it does little good to interfere. I have a feeling that nature will take care of what needs to be done."

Even as Dr. Key said it, a gust of wind picked up a cloud of sand from the beach and blew it into the wedding party, forcing the group to move indoors where they hurriedly finished the ceremony, and then headed to shelter.

"At least they'll have a wedding-day story to tell their children," Thermo said.

"Time for you to get out of there too, Thermo," instructed the doctor.

Thermo turned his jets on high and flew up and away from Florida, leaving the battered state behind, as the last of Phoon's billion-dollar hurricanes of 2004 swept over the peninsula.

In the real world, the 2004 hurricane season brought 3,270 deaths and more than 57 billion dollars in damage across the Caribbean into the United States. The "Fearsome Foursome" of Charley, Frances, Ivan and Jeanne did enough damage in Florida to force insurance companies to raise rates well above what they had been prior to 2004. Scientists continue to debate whether or not the frequency of hurricanes and their strength is affected by climate change. One thing is certain: the coastline of the U.S. is becoming more vulnerable, due primarily to the rapid buildup of both infrastructure and population since the mid-twentieth century. Also, due to sea level rise, coastlines are becoming more susceptible to the ill effects of tropical cyclones.

STORY 31: KATRINA

It was now the summer of 2005 and Phoon was still basking in the glow of a record-breaking Atlantic hurricane season the year before.

"I'm only getting warmed up!" Phoon shouted to the wind, "and with Carbo's help, I'll show the world what I can really do!"

Phoon's claims were not empty. After two tropical storms and a hurricane early in the season, Phoon unleashed its fury with Hurricane Dennis, slamming into the Florida panhandle and bringing widespread flooding as it moved inland. Two more hurricanes and four tropical storms followed, setting the stage for Phoon's crowning glory, and an unprecedented disaster.

It took the name of Katrina.

Dr. Key watched the events unfold from his laboratory on Mauna Loa. "Just look at that, Thermo," he said, pointing to a photo taken by a satellite orbiting the Earth. "This massive hurricane takes up practically half of the Gulf of Mexico. No one is crying wolf now."

"What do you mean, sir?" Thermo asked.

"Last year a lot of forecasters thought Hurricane Ivan might be a disaster for New Orleans," Dr. Key explained. "I fear that many people there in the city have chosen not to evacuate this time because of that previous mistake. New Orleans will certainly be hurt this time around, and I need you to be my eyes and ears when Katrina makes landfall. You'd better go now. And remember," the doctor warned, "Phoon is too strong for you to battle."

"I understand," Thermo said as he turned his jets on high and headed east toward the Gulf Coast.

His first stop was Biloxi, Mississippi, and the thermometer was shocked at what he saw there. Phoon's winds had already leveled entire neighborhoods. Whole buildings on the coast were now piles of rubble.

"The damage is incredible!" Thermo reported to Dr. Key over the two-way radio.

"I'm afraid we haven't seen the worst yet in New Orleans," Dr. Key replied. "Even though the wind is subsiding, the domed football stadium is full of people who sought shelter there, and the city's levee system is under a terrific strain. You'd better go take a look."

Thermo took off and sailed over to New Orleans. What he saw there was nothing short of pandemonium. The hurricane's surge of water against the city's floodwalls was breaching the levees, allowing water to pour into the city's 9th Ward neighborhood. "This is terrible, Dr. Key!"

"Yes, I can see the images through your camera eyes," the doctor lamented. "Keep moving."

Thermo continued to beam back the dreadful pictures of the scenes around him. He scanned the landscape and found water up to the roofs of countless homes. Entire families stood on their rooftops, surrounded by water and holding banners on which they had hand painted their pleas for help.

"Dr. Key!" Thermo shouted. "Would you be able to contact someone to help these people? You could give my location and maybe someone could send a rescue helicopter."

"Yes, Thermo, I'm contacting the authorities now."

Just then, Thermo's cumulus cloud buddies Puffy and Fluffy showed up. "Can we help, Thermo?" they offered.

"Oh boy, are you ever a sight for sore eyes!" whooped an excited Thermo. "It would help so much if you could drift over these homes and let me know where you see people in trouble."

"Look there!" yelled Fluffy, pointing to a small house a few hundred yards away. On the roof were a young man and young woman waving their arms and shouting. The woman was holding a crying baby and another small child sat nearby, shaking with fear. They all looked exhausted.

"Give me their location, Puffy!" shouted Thermo, and when he had the coordinates, he radioed them back to Dr. Key in Hawaii. In minutes a helicopter whirred overhead, on its way to the scared and stranded family.

Thermo, Puffy and Fluffy continued their diligent search-and-rescue efforts all day long, watching as dozens of individuals, couples and families were plucked from rooftops throughout the city. Now and then they spotted others struggling in the flood waters below, and with Dr. Key's help, guided rescue boats to their locations.

'We're making progress," Puffy said optimistically.

"Yes, we are," Fluffy agreed, "but so many people have already perished, and there are many others who still need help. It's impossible to save everyone."

"We are little," Thermo said softly, "and nature is big."

It was true, and try as they might, the trio knew there were hundreds who would not survive Katrina's flooding.

Dr. Key, try as he might, knew that with Carbo on the loose and getting stronger, Katrina would not be the last monster storm, not for this hurricane season, nor for future seasons either.

In the real world, Hurricane Katrina was one of the five deadliest hurricanes in U.S. history. Many meteorologists and most climatologists agreed that global warming enhanced Katrina's strength and helped produce the record number of tropical cyclones that year.

The 2005 hurricane season was the most active season on record for the Atlantic basin. Of the hurricanes that made landfall, five of the season's seven major hurricanes—Dennis, Emily, Katrina, Rita, and Wilma—were responsible for most of the destruction. Katrina was only the eleventh named storm out of a record twenty-eight tropical and subtropical storms that year. A record fifteen of those became hurricanes. 2005 was also notable because for the first time, the list of storm names was exhausted, and six Greek letter names had to be used. Tropical Storm Zeta became the final storm of the season when it formed on December 30.

Story 32: Invasion

Thermo cracked open the door to the laboratory at Mauna Loa. "Father?" he called. "Are you here?" Thermo listened, but there was only the whirring sound of the doctor's hard drives and the flickering of the computer monitors.

"Is that you, Thermo?" Dr. Key's butler Joshua stepped into the room. "I'm afraid Dr. Key is still in bed again. He has not been feeling well, and like so many other days, he just couldn't bring himself to do any work today."

"Tell me, Joshua," asked Thermo, "how sick is he?"

Joshua looked at the floor, paused, and then whispered, "It's not good, Thermo. He's getting older you know, and besides, there are some very nasty-looking moles on his legs. You know how much he loved to be in the sun. I am afraid it may have taken its toll."

"May I see him?" Thermo asked softly.

"Yes, I'll take you," answered Joshua.

As Thermo tiptoed into Dr. Key's room, the doctor opened his eyes. "Ah, Thermo my boy, I'm so sorry I am not up to my usual self."

"That's okay, Father. You'll be back to normal in no time."

"I'm afraid not, Son. I have some bad news. It's skin cancer and," he hesitated, then drew a breath and continued, "unfortunately I have only a few weeks to live."

The shock made Thermo so light-headed he could barely speak. "Wh-what?"

"Don't worry, Son, there's nothing to fret about. Something like this happens to us all sooner or later. But I would like to talk with Dr. Geoffrey White again. Could you call him for me?"

Dr. White arrived in Mauna Loa within days. Joshua led him to Dr. Key's room, and opening the door, the young scientist was greeted by a bleary-eyed Thermo sitting next to his maker's bed. A plastic tube ran from the doctor's nose to an oxygen tank. Dr. Key opened his eyes and smiled weakly. "Hello, White old boy. Good to see you."

The two scientists talked softly and measuredly, sometimes with long pauses so Dr. Key could catch his breath.

After a few minutes, their slow and labored conversation was interrupted by a sudden commotion in the rooms downstairs. Alarmed, Joshua and Thermo rushed from the bedroom, followed quickly by Dr. White.

What they saw at the bottom of the stairs was as terrifying as it was otherworldly. A small army of Hawaiian men stood before Dr. White, Thermo and Joshua with twisted and agonized looks on their faces. One of them, through a tortuous expression, managed a few words. "We are...being...controlled against our will by...C-C-Carbo!"

"Carbo!" Thermo and Dr. White shouted together.

"He has discovered our lab!" wailed Joshua.

Suddenly, one of the Hawaiians kicked wildly at Dr. White's head, missing it by a fraction of an inch.

"I recognize that move!" shouted Joshua. "It's Kapu Kuialua, a Hawaiian martial art!" Two more men moved toward Thermo and Joshua, while a whole group of men, bearing bundles of explosives, advanced toward Dr. White.

"It's just like at Mount Pinatubo!" cried Thermo. "And Carbo's henchmen are in control!"

"Right you are, little flying machine," announced Carbo's minion Toasty, appearing out of nowhere.

"Don't call me little!" screamed Thermo, jetting toward Toasty in a blind rage.

Toasty easily dodged Thermo's clumsy advance, sending the flying thermometer crashing into the wall of the lab and landing dazed on the floor.

Toasty exploded in laughter. "You're history, Mr. Thermometer! And with the help of my friends Roasty and Ghosty, these martial arts experts are going to blow this little headquarters of yours sky high. That ought to put a dent in your interference with Carbo's affairs!"

With that, one of the Hawaiians kicked and punched at Joshua. To the amazement of Thermo and Dr. White, Joshua kicked and punched back. Apparently the ordinarily sedate butler was also highly skilled in Kapu Kuialua.

Carbo's minion Ghosty took up the fight, flying toward Joshua's face in a furious effort to cut off the butler's oxygen supply. As Joshua struggled, Dr. White reached up above the fireplace and, pulling down an old-fashioned whale harpoon, hurled it at Ghosty. The harpoon found its mark, and the carbon dioxide molecule popped like a balloon, breaking into three pieces, two oxygen atoms and a single carbon atom, now drifting harmlessly in the air.

"Thanks," Joshua gasped, starting to breathe again.

Thermo finally pulled himself from the floor to resume the fight, but quickly realized he and Joshua and Dr. White were outnumbered. Back to Dr. Key's bedroom!" he shouted, and the three retreated, with the martial arts experts close behind.

Once back inside Dr. Key's room, Joshua instantly locked the door behind them, but everyone knew that it was only a temporary measure.

"There's a secret passage behind that bookcase," panted Joshua, pointing to a heavy cabinet. "It's what Dr. Key uses to get to the top of Mauna Loa to take his daily CO_2 readings. There's an electrical switch that moves the bookcase out of the way."

Turning to Dr. Key, Joshua urged, "We need to escape, sir. Carbo has hypnotized a small army down there. They have explosives. Please let me help you out of bed."

Just then came angry shouts and a violent pounding on the door. Dr. Key's face was ashen. "No, Joshua," the doctor said breathlessly. "I am too weak, and you don't have much time. This place could blow any moment. Now go!"

The pounding on the door grew stronger, and men and machine could hear the sound of wood splitting. Aghast, Joshua, Dr. White and Thermo looked at one another, and for the first time in his life, Thermo realized that he could shed tears.

Joshua was weeping too. He turned back to Dr. Key and shot a pleading look, but before he could speak, the doctor said firmly, "Goodbye Joshua. Goodbye Thermo. If my sensors on the volcano survive, please continue to take daily CO_2 readings. Finish my work. Keep up the fight. Defeat Carbo."

"We will Father," Thermo assured his dear maker through stifled sobs.

"This way!" Joshua directed, as he hit the switch to slide the heavy bookcase away from the door of their escape route.

Nothing happened.

"They've cut the power!" yelled Dr. White. "Help me move the bookcase!"

Joshua and Dr. White struggled and strained against the massive cabinet, but the two men couldn't budge it.

Quickly, Thermo flew into action. Wedging his miniature body between the bookcase and the wall, he used his jets to push against the weight of the shelves until a space opened, one just big enough for a man to squeeze through.

Just then, the bolted door crashed to the floor and the martial arts experts rushed into the room. Joshua and Dr. White pushed through the passageway. Thermo turned his jets on high, creating a dense cloud of smoke, burning the eyes of the Hawaiian captives and rendering them helpless. Thermo spun around, and without looking back, shot into the passageway.

As the two men and the little thermometer made their exit into daylight, they heard an explosion and deep rumble below.

"They've detonated the explosive charges!" Thermo cried. He instinctively grabbed each man by a single hand and, adjusting his jets to full throttle, soared upward with the men in tow, barely escaping the collapse of the mountain hideout.

Later, as the three sat in silent grief under the shade of a palm tree, Dr. White finally spoke. "Thank you for saving us, Thermo. If it weren't for your quick thinking and your small size, we wouldn't have made it out in time."

"My small size?" asked the little thermometer, blinking away a tear. "What do you mean?"

"You were the only one who could squeeze open a space behind the bookcase," said Joshua. "Thank goodness you are so little."

Thermo lowered his swollen eyes. There was that word again.

"In fact, your size has helped in so many ways over the years," said Dr. White. "Because you are so small, you were able to move quickly around the world to report on storms and rising temperatures."

"And help rescue people from the floods during Hurricane Katrina," added Joshua.

"And also give me a little peek inside the ethanol distillery at that cornfield," said Dr. White, smiling warmly.

Thermo thought for a moment. Finally he spoke. "I guess being little can sometimes be a pretty big advantage."

"Yes, and it's why I need you," Dr. White said gently. "I would like to continue Dr. Key's research."

"I am at your service, Dr. White," said Thermo.

Carbo had won still another battle. But the war was not over. Now, inspired by Dr. Key's sacrifice, Thermo was more determined than ever to see his creator's work completed.

In the real world, Dr. Joseph Keeling passed away in 2005. His Mauna Loa observatory has never been attacked, and as of this writing, CO_2 observations continue to be taken there. For the first time, during the 2013 Northern Hemisphere winter, official CO_2 accumulations reached levels of nearly 400 parts per million, and have since risen even higher.

STORY 33: THE NEW FRIEND

By the end of 2005, Thermo had noticed the increasing warmth across planet Earth. His new advisor and confidant Dr. Geoffrey White noticed it too.

"Heat waves are becoming more common, Thermo," the doctor told him. "Glaciers and arctic ice are in full retreat. Average worldwide temperatures are on the increase almost every year."

"Yes," said Thermo, "my latest readings confirm that. It's just as Dr. Key expected. Carbo is staying very busy."

Thermo and Dr. White sat together in the laboratory of the doctor's secluded cave in the hills of Pennsylvania. More than simply a home and lab, it was the perfect place for the young thermometer to unwind and grieve over the death of his creator Dr. Emmanuel Key. Thermo was grateful for Dr. White's invitation to stay with him, finding solace in the peaceful pastoral setting and in Dr. White's many animal companions. With so many climate scientists now out on dangerous missions, the doctor had volunteered to keep their pets while they were away. On any day there might be cats, horses, parakeets and even reptiles around the cave. Thermo's favorite was a Labrador retriever named Gladys, whose owner was a scientist currently studying the effects of climate change in Europe's Alps. Thermo and the dog had become fast friends, spending playful afternoons chasing one another and playing fetch.

Dr. White was also quickly becoming a new mentor to Thermo, and every day the two reminisced about the many assignments Thermo had performed for Dr. Key. They talked about the trips to faraway places with cloud pals Puffy and Fluffy; they laughed together about Snowy the snowman and his young friends Nicky and Sydney. Together they continually marveled at Thermo's narrow escapes from Skates the Ice Monster, Twista the Tornado and even Phoon the Hurricane, and speculated about when Heatia the Heat Monster might reappear.

From this remote location, Thermo and Dr. White also began to notice the subtle changes taking place in nature: more greenery growing at higher altitudes, more wild animals moving to higher ground, and pesky new insects flying around the cave during warmer summers.

"You know that I am determined to continue Dr. Key's work, Thermo," said Dr. White, "and I would like to continue to use your data as you travel the Earth. Would you help me in the growing battle against Carbo and his minions?"

"Of course," Thermo reassured the doctor, "but without Dr. Key…" Thermo's voice broke.

"Yes, it is a great loss," Dr. White said softly. "I miss him too, but we need to build on his work. We'll need more data than ever before, and we'll need it faster than ever if we're going to defeat Carbo."

I will do my best, Dr. White," said Thermo, "but there is only one of me."

Dr. White's face became more serious. "What if you had help, Thermo? What if there was someone else like you who could explore the world?"

"That would be wonderful! But Dr. Key told me the unusual way I was created, how it was a once-in-a-lifetime miracle. So I don't think it could ever happen again."

Dr. White stood and removed a large leather-bound volume from the top shelf of a large bookcase lining one wall of the cave. "This is a manuscript Dr. Key gave me before his laboratory was destroyed," he said, opening the book. "On these pages is the story of how you came to be. I've been studying it."

Thermo's eyes widened. "He wrote about how I was born?"

"Yes," said Dr. White, "and after some careful study and a bit of experimentation, I have been able to repeat the process."

It took a moment for Dr. White's statement to sink in.

"What are you saying, Doctor?" Thermo asked, mystified.

"I'm saying that I have created a friend for you, someone else like you, who can help gather more temperature data and speed up our work. Come here and I'll show you."

Dr. White stepped toward a closed door and motioned toward it. "Come on, Thermo," he encouraged. "I think you'll be pleased."

Thermo nervously rose from his chair and walked with Dr. White toward the door. The doctor reached up and gently knocked, calling, "May we come in?"

"Yes," came an almost musical voice from the other side. As Dr. White opened the door, Thermo's jaw dropped, and the thermometer on his chest rose a few degrees. There, sitting at a desk in front of a computer screen, was another living thermometer, someone just like him. No, not quite like him; the creature was indeed a thermometer with cameras for eyes and metal tubing for arms and legs, but there was more. The eyes were gentler. The head was shinier and softer, like threads made of gold. And the mouth—it was a little fuller, with more color. Thermo realized he was looking at the most beautiful creature he had ever laid camera-eyes on.

As he stared, the other thermometer continued to work, not looking up from her computer screen. "What can I do for you, Dr. White?" she asked.

Dr. White smiled at Thermo, who was both dumbfounded and enchanted. "Thermo, I'd like you to meet someone. This is Therma. She will be your new friend and helper."

Thermo was speechless. After an awkward silence, the female thermometer looked up, and with a little laugh asked, "What's the matter, Buster? Cat got your tongue?"

Thermo only continued to stare.

Unruffled, the new friend smiled, shook her head and looked back toward her computer screen. "It's nice to finally meet you too, Thermo," she chuckled, and then added faintly, "You have a pretty big reputation, considering you don't talk."

In that moment Thermo realized that after all the danger he had experienced, after all the missions he had accomplished, after all the science he had learned and all the experiments he had been a part of, his life had suddenly become bigger than he ever imagined.

END

In the real world, climatologists and environmentalists have documented invasive plants and animals moving into higher elevations over the past few years. Mosquitoes are biting later into the autumn season, bringing more threat of disease. Some animals such as the polar bear cannot adapt well to a warming world and could die out before the century is over.

Our story ends in 2005, when, in the real world, most scientists were coming out of "hiding," shedding more light on the climate problem without fear of retribution. Even now the climate story is still ongoing, and there is still much more scientific information to communicate and much misinformation yet to overcome. It is this author's hopeful opinion that truth, however dire or inconvenient it is, will eventually prevail, and our world's reliance on carbon-based fuels will one day be relegated to history.

APPENDIX

Story 1

Of course thermometers cannot fly, but recently many scientists have proposed that drones be built to take weather readings inside hurricanes, tropical storms and even tornadoes. The creation of Thermo by a lightning bolt is pure fiction. As far as we know, no force of nature is capable of bringing inanimate objects to life. But wouldn't it be fun if it could?

Story 3

The burning of fossil fuels since the advent of the Industrial Revolution has caused levels of CO_2 to steadily rise, threatening life as we know it. The reason Carbo can "think" and "feel" in our story when most other CO_2 molecules cannot is because carbon released by the burning of fossil fuels actually has a subtly different chemistry than that already in the atmosphere before the Industrial Revolution. That is one of the ways climate scientists are able to trace the growing amount of carbon pollution in the air.

In a process called photosynthesis, plants take in carbon dioxide from the air, water from the soil, and energy from sunlight to make the plants' food. During the process, plants release oxygen into the air. That is why Carbo needs to stay away from plants.

Story 5

Hurricane expert Dr. John Hope, whom this author considers to be The Weather Channel's founding father of tropical meteorology, had a daughter named Camille. While working at the National Hurricane Center, he added her name to the list of names to be used for hurricanes that year. He had no idea that the storm named after his daughter would become one of the most powerful hurricanes in history. Shortly after I was hired at The Weather Channel, the first major tropical system we covered, Hurricane Alicia, slammed ashore directly into the Houston/Galveston, Texas area in August of 1983. It was a category three hurricane with winds of 115 mph. Television coverage of Alicia gave increased scientific credibility to The Weather Channel and caused its ratings to soar. In fact, before Alicia in the mid-1980s, the network was close to permanently going off the air. Dr. Hope worked countless sleepless hours giving the public the latest information on Alicia, and was truly a meteorological hero. I also worked with a little-known graphics technician named Andrew Colletti who endured double shifts to keep John Hope's graphics fresh and updated. Andrew was himself a true behind-the-scenes hero during coverage of Alicia. To this day, because of the credibility garnered from the coverage of Alicia, The Weather Channel has high ratings when tropical systems threaten the United States. Dr. John Hope was The Weather Channel's chief tropical expert until his death in June of 2002.

Story 6

The molecules in ice crystals join to one another in a six-sided structure to give snowflakes their familiar shape, but in the coldest temperatures, snowflakes look more like thin plates, needles or hollow columns. Typically, temperatures must be below 15 degrees Fahrenheit for flurries to form in cumulus clouds, though they can fall through somewhat warmer air and reach the ground where air temperatures are as high as the upper 30s to low 40s. During outbreaks of arctic temperatures, cumulus clouds can bring flurries even into the southern United States.

Story 7

Climate scientists believe the burning of coal, oil and gas in the 20th century is responsible for the rise of average temperatures over the globe. The consensus of climate scientists is that in order for the current climate of the planet to stabilize, the level of carbon in the atmosphere needs to remain at 350 parts per million. At this writing, current atmospheric observations from Mauna Loa indicate that roughly 406 parts per million of carbon dioxide is in the atmosphere, and that the number is still rising.

One climate scientist hero who recommends the 350-ppm figure is Bill McKibben. You can get more information about his efforts and learn how to support greater use of renewable energy at www.350.org

Story 8

This author was an eleven-year-old child during the Great Ice Storm of 1973, living in the small town of Tignall, Georgia. The area was hit hard by the storm. I remember that due to power outages, people stored their frozen food outside to keep it from spoiling. I was happy to be out of school, but quickly bored from hovering near a fireplace for days with only a couple of books to read. As I recall, none of the TV meteorologists at the time expected the storm, most calling only for a cold rain across north Georgia. Nowadays, computer models would forecast an ice storm like the one in 1973 at least 48 hours in advance.

An ice storm of such magnitude over north Georgia today would be much more catastrophic. Since 1973, the population of metropolitan Atlanta has grown from less than two million people to more than five and a half million. Unfortunately, some parts of the power line infrastructure have not changed much since the early 70s, and two-to-three inches of ice and sleet would surely cause massive outages. Even though worldwide temperatures now average about a degree-and-a-half warmer (Fahrenheit) than in the early 70s, it is too early to write off another ice storm for the Deep South.

Story 9

The snowstorm that struck February 9-10, 1973 was one of the oddest meteorological systems in this author's memory. Temperatures during the event the night of February 9 through 10 were in the 20s F. The snow was not the typical wet snow that falls across the South, but a fine powder. Once again, the weather forecasters at the time had a hard time accurately forecasting the intensity of the storm.

As an eleven-year-old boy I was delighted to play in the white stuff. I made some big snowmen with my younger sister Dorothy. I remember a couple, Mr. and Mrs. Smith, who had moved south from Michigan to my town of Tignall, Georgia in order to farm some land. They got out their old (and what they thought would be stored forever) sleigh and hooked it up to some horses. The Smiths delighted the children of Tignall with long rides the afternoon of February 10. The storm dumped twelve inches of snow on Tignall and remains one of my favorite childhood memories.

Story 10

Svante August Arrhenius was not the only scientist of his day familiar with the greenhouse effect. In 2016, documents were discovered that indicated the first scientist to identify the greenhouse effect was Eunice Foote in 1857. Irish physicist John Tyndall is commonly credited for discovering the greenhouse effect in 1859, which laid the foundation for the science of climate change, but it would appear that Eunice Foote beat him to it.

Story 11

To this date there is no real correlation between the number and intensity of tornadoes and global warming, although it appears that tornado outbreaks are beginning to occur "out of season." In other words, some tornadoes are developing across areas that typically would be too cold for storms, given the time of the year. Such was more recently the case with the November 17, 2014 outbreak across Illinois and Indiana.

The real heroes during the April 3-4, 1974 "Super Outbreak" were the many men and women of the National Weather Service (called the U.S. Weather Bureau before 1970) along the path of the storms. The first weather radio broadcast was from Los Angeles in 1967. By the time of the 1974 outbreak there was a fairly large network of Weather Service offices broadcasting forecasts, watches and warnings using the NOAA Weather Radio system. Though more than 300 people died in the outbreak, many others were saved due to timely issuance of warnings, although it was not until the widespread use of Doppler radar after 1988 that warnings proved more accurate and provided more lead time. Before that, the Weather Service's rudimentary radar detected tornadoes mainly by their hook-shaped echoes, though not every tornado produces one. 1974's Super Outbreak convinced government authorities to plan and build the Doppler radar network, which today saves countless lives.

Story 13

In 1971, climatologist Stephen Schneider published his opinion that increased air pollution would cool the Earth. After further research and peer review, Schneider recanted his findings in 1975, admitting that he had overestimated the cooling effects of pollution on the atmosphere, and had underestimated the warming effects of carbon dioxide. The scientific method is a crucible of truth, allowing scientists to correct one another's errors, even their own.

This author remembers back to high school days in the late 1970s when there were two very cold back-to-back winters, 1976 to 1977 and 1977 to 1978. It was so cold in January of 1977 that some of the school systems in the Atlanta area closed for a week due to a lack of natural gas. Low temperatures in Atlanta got into the single digits several times from November 1976 to January 1977. Numerous record lows were set across the eastern U.S. and President Carter's inauguration in January 1977 was one of the coldest inaugural ceremonies in U.S. history. It is no wonder that some climatologists and the public thought that an ice age was imminent.

Time Magazine even did a headline story on the "coming ice age" that climate change opponents still propagate to this day.

Story 14

Two of the reasons this author became a meteorologist were the heat wave of 1980 and Hurricane Allen in the Gulf of Mexico. Allen reached Category 5 intensity, becoming the earliest Category 5 hurricane ever recorded in the Atlantic Basin at that time. It was also the only hurricane in the Atlantic basin to record sustained winds of 190 mph. In addition, Allen's legacy included squelching the heat and high pressure in south Texas that August.

Was global warming already producing both a nearly unprecedented heat wave and a hurricane as early as 1980? Clearly, the atmosphere from Mexico and the Caribbean northward into the U.S. was very warm that summer. More recently, record heat in the summer (and winter in the southern hemisphere) was present from Australia northward into China in 2013. The western Pacific saw numerous strong typhoons, including the record-setting Typhoon Haiyan, which crossed over the central Philippines during the fall later that year. Was it just another coincidence, or was it something else?

Story 15

A group of Iranian students took over the American Embassy in Tehran in November 1979, holding 52 American diplomats hostage for 444 days, the longest hostage crisis in history. A failed military attempt to rescue them in April, 1980 is seen by political analysts as one of the reasons for Jimmy Carter's unsuccessful reelection bid and his opponent Ronald Reagan's landslide victory a few months later. Negotiators finally secured their release on January 20, 1981, the same day Reagan was sworn in as new President.

There is strong evidence that the Saudis and other foreign oil-producing interests tried to keep oil prices low and the oil spigots flowing during the 1980s. In fact, due to discoveries and drilling innovations, the price of crude oil fell so much that the Organization of the Petroleum Exporting Countries (OPEC) of which Saudi Arabia is a part, had to cut production to maintain profits. The price of fossil fuels became so low that there was almost no need for conservation from Reagan's presidency through the end of the 20th century. Due to a lack of consensus in the 1980s about how bad global warming could eventually get, historians can probably excuse Reagan for his actions; however, they may not be as forgiving toward today's leaders.

Story 16

Despite misgivings from many congressional leaders, Dr. James Hansen's testimony in 1988 put the threat of global warming in the forefront of public recognition. Dr. Hansen was instrumental in convincing this author of the real threat from carbon pollution. Check out his first book published in 2009, *Storms of My Grandchildren*. It paints a dim picture of the future of humanity, should carbon emissions go unchecked.

Story 17

One environmentalist who was killed because of his environmental advocacy was "Doc" Gerry Ortega of the Philippines. In March, 2011 Mr. Ortega was shot while browsing in a second-hand clothing store in Puerto Princesa, the capital of the Palawan province. Ortega made enemies on his daily radio show, accusing politicians of corruption and of allowing the island's natural resources to be pillaged. Palawan has been called the "last ecological frontier of the Philippines," and Ortega's death is an example of the struggle across that country, where, according to the organization Global Witness, at least fifty environmental campaigners have been killed over the past decade.

Story 18

The eruption of Mt Pinatubo on June 15, 1991 killed 847 people and destroyed more than 8,000 homes. In all, 364 communities were impacted by the eruption. Of course, simple explosives can't set off an earthquake; massive internal pressure within the Earth's crust produces the fissures that lead to volcanoes. The effects of the 1991 eruption were felt worldwide, as average temperatures fell by about one degree Fahrenheit over the next year. Some meteorologists at the time discounted man-made climate change because of the worldwide cooling from the eruption.

Story 19

Andrew, the first named storm of the 1992 Atlantic Hurricane Season, became a tropical storm on August 17, very late for an "A" named storm. Not long after, the storm began weakening because of increased wind shear from the southwest. Hurricane Hunter crews could no longer locate a well-defined center in Andrew and measured rapidly rising air pressure readings. Almost as quickly, Andrew regained strength after wind shear decreased over the storm, quickly becoming more organized and reaching hurricane status on August 22.

The center of Andrew brought sustained winds of 165 mph to Homestead Florida. Although Miami did not receive a direct blow, there was severe damage throughout South Florida, making Andrew, at the time, the costliest hurricane to strike the United States. After moving over Florida, Andrew made a second landfall in southern Louisiana with winds of 115 mph.

The meteorologists in the Hurricane Hunter fleet are nothing less than meteorological heroes. Some who flew missions before 1990 literally risked their lives in older planes. The modern fleet of hurricane planes now has very little chance of going down, even while monitoring the most powerful of storms. There are two groups of Hurricane Hunters; one is a part of the National Oceanic and Atmospheric Administration, and another is from the U.S. Air Force Reserve.

Bryan Norcross (Steven Woods in our story) was a hurricane expert at The Weather Channel for several years. Check out his book on his experience in Florida, *My Hurricane Andrew Story.*

Story 20

The "Storm of the Century" (or "1993 Superstorm" or the "Great Blizzard of 1993") formed over the Gulf of Mexico on March 12 and dissipated in the North Atlantic Ocean on March 15. The storm was unique for its intensity, massive size and wide-reaching effects. At its height, the powerful storm stretched from Canada southward toward Central America, but its main impact was felt in the Eastern United States.

This author was impressed with the storm while living in downtown Atlanta. It was the first time that I had ever experienced a true blizzard, with winds of over 40 mph and snow piling as high as a foot. Storm totals across the city ranged from four inches at Atlanta's airport south of the city, to as much as 16 inches on the north side in Marietta. For the first time in my life I saw thunder snow, when heavy rain changed over to heavy snow on the morning of the 12th. Also for the first time, I saw frozen daffodil blooms in the middle of March as temperatures dropped to between ten and fifteen degrees Fahrenheit.

At the time, some scientists wondered if there was a connection between the unusual weather pattern that led to the Storm of the Century and the two-to-three-year global cooling due to the eruption of Mount Pinatubo. Such a connection has never been established.

Story 21

Dendrochronology was developed during the first half of the 20th century originally by astronomer A. E. Douglass, the founder of the Laboratory of Tree-Ring Research at the University of Arizona. Douglass sought to better understand cycles of sunspot activity, and reasoned that changes in solar activity would affect climate patterns on earth, which would subsequently be recorded by tree-ring growth patterns.

Story 22

Climatologists have been watching and recording glaciers for several decades because they are a good barometer of warming or cooling trends. Measurements from Kilimanjaro have received the most press, and indicate that the Earth's climate is warming at an increasingly high rate into the 21st century.

Story 23

Until the 1997-98 El Niño, the 1982-83 El Niño was one of the strongest in recorded history. The impacts in the early 80s included heavy rain and flooding on the Pacific coast of South America, in California, along the U.S. Gulf Coast, in Eastern Europe, and in East Africa. Drought and wildfires spread throughout Australia, Southeast Asia, Mexico, Central America, Texas, Florida, and northeastern Brazil. Strong hurricanes swept through the eastern Pacific and typhoons buffeted the western Pacific.

Then came the El Niño of 1997–98. Its impacts were similar to the 1982-83 event. In addition, more acres of tropical rain forest burned than at any other time in recorded history through the end of the 20th century. By the time the episode ended in May 1998, the worldwide death toll due to El Niño-related weather was near 23,000, and property damage totaled well over thirty billion dollars.

To the best of this author's knowledge, carbon pollution does not directly affect the frequency of El Niños or La Niñas, but many climate scientists believe that a warming Earth could produce more frequent and stronger El Niños. After a big spike in global temperature averages in 1998, there has been a warming trend, but not so much that those who deny global warming from carbon pollution have recanted their positions. The El Nino of 2015-16, which was nearly as strong as that of 1997-98, was a catalyst that spiked global temperatures to unprecedented levels in 2016.

Story 24

The North American Ice Storm that struck parts of Canada and the northeastern United States in January of 1998 was a combination of five smaller ice storms, one after another. The system caused widespread damage to trees and power lines throughout the area, leading to pervasive and long-lasting power outages. Millions were left without electricity for weeks, and in some cases, months. The storm killed 35 people and shut down normal activity in many large cities including Ottawa and Montreal. More than 16,000 Canadian Forces troops were called in during the storm, the largest deployment of the Canadian military since the Korean War. This author speculates that in the absence of a warming world, the ice storm would have occurred much farther south.

Story 25

Dr. Michael Mann's Hockey Stick Graph has become a symbol to environmentalists of what can happen to the planet if greenhouse gasses remain unchecked. The most comprehensive and fully independent climate reconstruction to date, the "Pages 2K Project," produced a virtually identical twin of the original Hockey Stick graph introduced almost 15 years earlier. Dr. Mann remains a climatologist hero for his efforts to slow climate change, and global temperature data continues to mirror much of Dr. Mann's work. In 2016 Dr. Mann published his book about climate science politics titled *The Madhouse Effect: How Climate Change Denial is Threatening our Planet, Destroying Our Politics, and Driving Us Crazy.*

Today's jet engines do produce greenhouse gases, including two percent of the world's manmade CO_2. The aviation industry is working to develop new engine designs and fuels to help reduce those emissions.

Story 26

In this author's opinion, the election of Bush along with a majority of Republicans in the House of Representatives prevented the United States from taking a leading role on the global warming front worldwide for at least a decade. One can only guess what would have happened if Al Gore had been elected President, but there is little doubt that the climate issue would have been more at the forefront. The new century began in the United States with an increasingly polarized public and an ever-widening chasm between those who recognized the problem of climate change and those determined to squelch its adherents.

Story 27

Hybrid cars were not a new idea at the beginning of the 21st century. Ferdinand Porsche developed the Lohner-Porsche Mixte Hybrid in 1901, but a popular hybrid-electric vehicle did not become widely available until the release of the Toyota Prius in Japan in 1997, followed by the Honda Insight in 1999.

Due to the low cost of fuel in the United States during the late 1990's, hybrids were slow to catch on. Worldwide increases in the price of oil caused many automakers to release hybrids in the late 2000s, and hybrids now make up a large segment of the automotive market.

It is this author's hope that reducing our world's dependence on fossil fuels will reduce the likelihood of a future war over energy resources.

Story 29

The 2003 European heat wave led to health crises in several countries and produced a devastating drought over southern Europe. On the positive side, the heat wave helped to change some energy policies in France, Germany, Spain and Italy. Most of the European countries were spurred to concentrate on producing more green non-carbon-based energy. This particular heat wave was so unusual that most climate scientists and meteorologists think that the event could not have occurred in the absence of an overall warming world.

Story 30

In 2004 this author attended a beach wedding the day before Hurricane Jeanne moved towards Tampa, Florida. Nicky, one of the children from my Snowy story is named for the son of the couple who married that day. Jeanne was forecast by computer models to move northwest along the east coast of Florida, but instead moved west-northwest through the heart of the state. Needless to say, the wedding celebration turned into a hurricane party (with no electricity) when Jeanne got close to Tampa on the 27th of September. Frances, Ivan and Jeanne produced flooding rain for most of the Southeast during August and September.

Story 31

This author was in his 23rd year as a forecaster for The Weather Channel during the record-breaking 2005 Atlantic hurricane season.

Awestruck by the size and strength of Katrina as it approached the central Gulf Coast, I noted at the time that before heading inland, the central pressure of the tropical cyclone had lowered to an amazing 922 millibars, abnormally deep for a hurricane making landfall along the Gulf Coast.

Hurricane Katrina strengthened to a category five hurricane over the warm Gulf waters, but weakened to a category three before making landfall on the Louisiana-Mississippi coast on August 29. Katrina caused widespread damage from central Florida to Texas, much of it due to storm surge flooding. New Orleans's levee system catastrophically failed, resulting in the most significant number of deaths from Katrina, numbering well above a thousand. Much of the city flooded, and even after Katrina weakened and moved inland, flooding lingered for weeks. The worst property damage occurred in coastal areas, such as in Mississippi beachfront towns. Boats washed up on shore, and buildings and homes were wiped away. Floodwaters reached a dozen miles inland.

The hurricane surge protection failure in New Orleans is considered the worst civil engineering disaster in U.S. history, prompting a lawsuit against the U.S. Army Corps of Engineers that designed and built the levee system. The administration of President George W. Bush endured finger pointing and blame due to what was perceived to be slow action in rescue operations and distribution of aid during the first week after Katrina's landfall.

Though many meteorologists and climatologists believe that the warmer-than-average atmosphere surrounding Hurricane Katrina allowed the hurricane to become much stronger than it would have otherwise, it is the educated opinion of this author that such conclusions are still premature, although I do think that the strength of 2012's Superstorm Sandy was enhanced by global warming, as well as its track toward the Northeastern U.S.

Story 32

Dr. Joseph Keeling died in 2005, but not from melanoma cancer. This author is familiar with the torment of melanoma, however. The disease took my own father in 2002. Regular use of sunscreen and frequent examinations from a dermatologist are important, especially for those who have endured frequent sun exposure or who have a family history of the disease. Thankfully there is no correlation between cases of skin cancer and increased carbon dioxide in the atmosphere. However, there is evidence that a depleted ozone layer in our atmosphere could lead to increased U-V radiation and as a result, more cases of skin cancer.

ABOUT THE AUTHOR

Guy Walton is a meteorologist and thirty-year veteran of The Weather Channel. He has forecast the major headline-making storms, including Hurricanes Andrew and Katrina, Superstorm Sandy and the Super Tornado Outbreak of 2011. He has spent several years meticulously cataloguing climate data from around the world, leading to the Meehl Surface Temperature Records Study, now used as a measure for climate change. Although a tragic fall a few years ago confined Guy to a wheelchair, he maintains a blog at GuyOnClimate.com with regular climate articles and research results.

67828576R00100

Made in the USA
Middletown, DE
12 September 2019